HARRAP'S

The Legend of Sleepy Hollow

WASHINGTON IRVING

and Other Scary Stories

BY ARTHUR CONAN DOYLE

AND EDGAR ALLAN POE

Pour les notes en marge du texte :

21, rue du Montparnasse
75283 Paris CEDEX 06

HARRAP's® est une marque de Larousse SAS
www.harrap.com

ISBN 978 2 81 870 692 3

About the authors

WASHINGTON IRVING (1783-1859) was an American writer and diplomat. The youngest of a large family, he studied law[1] and passed the bar examination[2] (1806) after a two-year grand tour of Western Europe. A successful fiction writer, he also researched and wrote biographies of Christopher Columbus and of his own namesake[3], George Washington. He knew how to draw from local folklore and is now hailed[4] as one of the first genuine American authors. His characters[5] Rip Van Winkle and Ichabod Crane are still household names[6] in America.

1. le droit
2. examen d'entrée au barreau
3. homonyme
4. salué
5. personnages
6. célèbres

SIR ARTHUR CONAN DOYLE (1859-1930) was born in Edinburgh and studied medecine. He had an active career as a doctor and ophtalmologist, including volunteering in South Africa during the Boer War (1899-1902) and the First World War.

It was for his brilliant creation of the first scientific detective, Sherlock Holmes (*A Study in Scarlet*, 1881) that he achieved great fame[7]. He later converted to spiritualism and was a friend of the magician Houdini.

7. connut une grande célébrité

EDGAR ALLAN POE (1809-1849) was born in Boston, Massachusetts (USA). Orphaned very early[8], he was sent to live with his uncle and aunt in Virginia. His short novel *Murders in the Rue Morgue* (1841) is considered the first modern detective story. Also known as a poet and indulgent literary critic, he was a master of the wild, the weird and the macabre.

8. Orphelin de bonne heure

DIRECTION DE LA PUBLICATION : Carine Girac-Marinier

NOTES EN MARGE : Delphine Nègre-Bouvet

RÉVISION DES NOTES : Marianne Mouchot

RELECTURE : F. Le Dantec

INFORMATIQUE ÉDITORIALE ET MISE EN PAGES :
Philippe Cazabet, Marie-Noëlle Tilliette

CONCEPTION GRAPHIQUE : Uli Meindl

FABRICATION : Rebecca Dubois

Mot de l'Éditeur

Vous aimeriez lire en langue originale, mais le vocabulaire, les expressions figurées ou la syntaxe vous arrêtent parfois ?

Cette collection est faite pour vous !

Vous trouverez en effet, en note dans la marge, une traduction de certains mots et expressions qui vous permettra d'avancer facilement dans votre lecture.

Nous n'avons pas cherché à vous donner une traduction littéraire de l'ouvrage et nous nous sommes parfois écartés du sens littéral pour vous fournir le sens qui convient le mieux à l'histoire. Aussi les mots sont-ils traduits dans le contexte du texte original.

Les expressions figées anglaises sont, bien entendu, rendues par une expression équivalente en français.

Les allusions à des réalités culturelles du monde anglo-saxon sont expliquées également dans la marge, pour vous aider à mieux comprendre la trame de l'histoire.

Vous aurez ainsi, en regard du texte original, tout le savoir-faire d'un dictionnaire rien que pour vous et adapté à ce livre !

Notre objectif est de vous mener jusqu'au mot FIN en vous donnant les clés nécessaires à la compréhension du récit.

Plongez dans ces récits nés de l'imagination fertile des maîtres anglo-saxons de l'étrange et de l'épouvante...

Lire en VO ? You can indeed!

Coup de pouce pour vous aider à bien comprendre le début de l'histoire…

Au nord de l'Amérique, près de la baie du fleuve auquel le navigateur Hudson a donné son nom, il est un vallon tranquille, si tranquille qu'il paraît sous l'emprise d'un charme étrange.

Descendants des colons hollandais, les habitants du vallon sont très superstitieux. Ou faut-il dire crédules ?

THE LEGEND OF SLEEPY HOLLOW[1]

by Washington Irving

1. Vallon

(Found Among the Papers of the Late[2] Dietrich Knickerbocker.)

2. feu

A pleasing land of drowsy head[3] it was,
Of dreams that wave[4] before the half-shut eye;
And of gay castles in the clouds that pass,
Forever flushing round[5] a summer sky.
Castle of Indolence

3. somnolence
4. ondulent
5. Tournoyant éternellement dans

In the bosom[6] of one of those spacious coves[7] which indent[8] the eastern shore[9] of the Hudson, at that broad expansion of the river denominated by the ancient Dutch navigators the Tappan Zee, and where they always prudently shortened sail[10] and implored the protection of St. Nicholas when they crossed, there lies[11] a small market town or rural port, which by some is called Greensburgh, but which is more generally and properly known by the name of Tarry[12] Town. This name was given, we are told, in former days[13], by the good housewives of the adjacent country, from the inveterate propensity[14] of their husbands to linger about[15] the village tavern on market days. Be that as it may[16], I do not vouch for the[17] fact, but merely

6. Au fond
7. criques
8. découpent
9. rive
10. réduisaient la voilure
11. se trouve
12. musardière
13. au temps jadis
14. fâcheuse tendance
15. s'attarder dans
16. Quoi qu'il en soit
17. ne réponds pas du

advert to it[1], for the sake of being[2] precise and authentic. Not far from this village, perhaps about two miles, there is a little valley or rather lap[3] of land among high hills, which is one of the quietest places in the whole world. A small brook[4] glides through it, with just murmur enough to lull one to repose[5]; and the occasional whistle of a quail[6] or tapping[7] of a woodpecker[8] is almost the only sound that ever breaks in upon[9] the uniform tranquillity.

I recollect[10] that, when a stripling[11], my first exploit in squirrel-shooting[12] was in a grove[13] of tall walnut-trees that shades one side of the valley. I had wandered into it[14] at noontime, when all nature is peculiarly quiet, and was startled by the roar of my own gun, as it broke the Sabbath stillness around[15] and was prolonged and reverberated by the angry echoes. If ever I should wish for a retreat whither I might steal from[16] the world and its distractions, and dream quietly away the remnant of a troubled life[17], I know of none[18] more promising than this little valley.

From the listless repose[19] of the place, and the peculiar character of its inhabitants, who are descendants from the original Dutch settlers[20], this sequestered glen[21] has long been known by the name of SLEEPY HOLLOW, and its rustic lads[22] are called the Sleepy Hollow Boys throughout all the neighboring country. A drowsy, dreamy influence seems to hang over the land, and to pervade the very atmosphere[23]. Some say that the place was bewitched[24] by a High German[25] doctor, during the early days of the settlement; others, that an old Indian chief, the prophet or wizard[26] of his tribe, held his powwows there[27] before the

1. l'indique simplement
2. par souci de me montrer
3. un bout
4. ruisseau
5. vous inciter au repos
6. caille
7. le tambourinement
8. pivert
9. vienne rompre
10. me souviens
11. tout jeune homme
12. de chasse à l'écureuil
13. bosquet
14. m'y étais enfoncé
15. qui rompait la quiétude dominicale
16. Si je cherche un jour une retraite où fuir
17. passer à rêvasser le reste de ma vie agitée
18. n'en connais pas de
19. En raison de l'indolence
20. colons hollandais
21. vallon isolé
22. campagnards
23. d'imprégner l'air qu'on y respire
24. ensorcelé
25. allemand
26. sorcier
27. y convoquait ses assemblées

country was discovered by Master Hendrick Hudson. Certain it is, the place still continues under the sway[1] of some witching power, that holds a spell over the minds of[2] the good people, causing them to walk in a continual reverie. They are given to[3] all kinds of marvellous beliefs, are subject to trances[4] and visions, and frequently see strange sights, and hear music and voices in the air. The whole neighborhood abounds with local tales[5], haunted spots[6], and twilight[7] superstitions; stars shoot[8] and meteors glare[9] oftener across the valley than in any other part of the country, and the nightmare[10], with her whole ninefold[11], seems to make it the favorite scene of her gambols[12].

The dominant spirit, however, that haunts this enchanted region, and seems to be commander-in-chief of all the powers of the air, is the apparition of a figure[13] on horseback, without a head. It is said by some to be the ghost of a Hessian trooper[14], whose head had been carried away[15] by a cannon-ball[16], in some nameless battle during the Revolutionary War, and who is ever and anon[17] seen by the country folk hurrying along in the gloom of night[18], as if on the wings of the wind. His haunts[19] are not confined to the valley, but extend at times to the adjacent roads, and especially to the vicinity[20] of a church at no great distance. Indeed, certain of the most authentic historians of those parts, who have been careful in collecting and collating[21] the floating[22] facts concerning this spectre, allege[23] that the body of the trooper having been buried in the churchyard, the ghost rides forth to[24] the scene of battle in nightly quest[25] of his head, and that the rushing speed with which he sometimes passes along

1. est toujours sous l'emprise
2. tient sous son charme
3. sujets à
4. en proie à des transes
5. légendes
6. en lieux hantés
7. crépusculaires
8. filent
9. brillent
10. démon de la nuit
11. et toute sa suite [cf. Shakespeare, *Le roi Lear* : « Il rencontra l'incube et ses neuf familiers »]
12. cabrioles
13. silhouette
14. soldat de la Hesse [en Allemagne]
15. emportée
16. boulet de canon
17. périodiquement
18. ténèbres
19. apparitions
20. aux alentours
21. recueillir
22. indécis
23. prétendent
24. chevauche vers
25. toutes les nuits à la recherche

1. explosion
2. due au fait qu'il est en retard
3. qu'il a hâte
4. l'aube
5. teneur
6. alimenté toutes sortes d'histoires folles
7. Cavalier sans tête
8. autochtones
9. gagne inconsciemment
10. Si éveillés qu'ils aient pu être
11. à devenir
12. les éloges possibles
13. car
14. au cœur du
15. qui ne tient pas en place
16. passe au large ni vu ni connu
17. recoins
18. stagnante
19. torrent
20. venir tranquillement aboutir
21. formant de lents tourbillons
22. baie miniature
23. se soient écoulées
24. que j'ai parcouru
25. me demande
26. si

the Hollow, like a midnight blast[1], is owing to his being belated[2], and in a hurry[3] to get back to the churchyard before daybreak[4].

Such is the general purport[5] of this legendary superstition, which has furnished materials for many a wild story[6] in that region of shadows; and the spectre is known at all the country firesides, by the name of the Headless Horseman[7] of Sleepy Hollow.

It is remarkable that the visionary propensity I have mentioned is not confined to the native inhabitants[8] of the valley, but is unconsciously imbibed by[9] every one who resides there for a time. However wide awake they may have been[10] before they entered that sleepy region, they are sure, in a little time, to inhale the witching influence of the air, and begin to grow[11] imaginative, to dream dreams, and see apparitions.

I mention this peaceful spot with all possible laud[12], for[13] it is in such little retired Dutch valleys, found here and there embosomed in the[14] great State of New York, that population, manners, and customs remain fixed, while the great torrent of migration and improvement, which is making such incessant changes in other parts of this restless[15] country, sweeps by them unobserved[16]. They are like those little nooks[17] of still[18] water, which border a rapid stream[19], where we may see the straw and bubble riding quietly at anchor[20], or slowly revolving[21] in their mimic harbor[22], undisturbed by the rush of the passing current. Though many years have elapsed[23] since I trod[24] the drowsy shades of Sleepy Hollow, yet I question[25] whether[26] I should not still find the same trees and the same families vegetating in its sheltered bosom[1].

In this by-place of nature[2] there abode[3], in a remote period of American history, that is to say, some thirty years since, a worthy wight[4] of the name of Ichabod Crane, who sojourned, or, as he expressed it, "tarried[5]," in Sleepy Hollow, for the purpose of instructing the children of the vicinity. He was a native[6] of Connecticut, a State which supplies the Union with pioneers for the mind as well as for the forest, and sends forth yearly[7] its legions of frontier woodmen and country schoolmasters. The cognomen[8] of Crane[9] was not inapplicable to his person. He was tall, but exceedingly lank[10], with narrow shoulders, long arms and legs, hands that dangled a mile out of his sleeves[11], feet that might have served for shovels[12], and his whole frame most loosely hung together[13]. His head was small, and flat at top, with huge ears, large green glassy eyes, and a long snipe[14] nose, so that it looked like a weather-cock[15] perched upon his spindle neck[16] to tell which way the wind blew. To see him striding along the profile of[17] a hill on a windy day, with his clothes bagging and fluttering about him[18], one might have mistaken him for the genius of famine descending upon the earth, or some scarecrow eloped[19] from a cornfield.

His schoolhouse was a low building of one large room, rudely constructed of logs[20]; the windows partly glazed[21], and partly patched[22] with leaves of old copybooks[23]. It was most ingeniously secured[24] at vacant hours, by a withe[25] twisted in the handle of the door, and stakes[26] set against the window shutters; so that though a thief might

1. sein abrité
2. site isolé,
3. demeurait
4. brave homme
5. musardait
6. originaire
7. envoie chaque année
8. nom de famille
9. [« la grue »]
10. efflanqué
11. dépassaient de beaucoup ses manches
12. de pelles
13. un corps tout dégingandé
14. de bécasse
15. girouette
16. tige
17. À le voir parcourir à grands pas
18. se gonflant et claquant
19. épouvantail échappé
20. grossier assemblage de rondins
21. vitrées
22. rapiécées
23. cahiers
24. verrouillée
25. brin d'osier
26. des pieux

get in with perfect ease, he would find some embarrassment in getting out,—an idea most probably borrowed by the architect, Yost Van Houten, from the mystery of an eelpot[1]. The schoolhouse stood in a rather lonely but pleasant situation, just at the foot of a woody hill, with a brook running close by[2], and a formidable birch-tree[3] growing at one end of it. From hence[4] the low murmur of his pupils' voices, conning over[5] their lessons, might be heard in a drowsy summer's day, like the hum[6] of a bee-hive[7]; interrupted now and then by the authoritative voice of the master, in the tone of menace or command, or, peradventure[8], by the appalling[9] sound of the birch[10], as he urged some tardy loiterer along[11] the flowery path of knowledge[12]. Truth to say, he was a conscientious man, and ever bore in mind the golden maxim, "Spare the rod and spoil the child."[13] Ichabod Crane's scholars certainly were not spoiled[14].

I would not have it imagined[15], however, that he was one of those cruel potentates of the school who joy in the smart[16] of their subjects; on the contrary, he administered justice with discrimination[17] rather than severity; taking the burden[18] off the backs of the weak, and laying it on those of the strong. Your mere puny stripling, that winced[19] at the least flourish[20] of the rod[21], was passed by[22] with indulgence; but the claims[23] of justice were satisfied by inflicting a double portion on some little tough wrong-headed, broad-skirted[24] Dutch urchin[25], who sulked[26] and swelled[27] and grew dogged and sullen[28] beneath the birch. All this he called "doing his duty by[29] their parents;" and he never inflicted a chastisement without following it by the assurance,

1. curieux mécanisme d'une nasse à anguilles
2. à deux pas d'un ruisseau
3. imposant bouleau
4. De là,
5. ressassant
6. bourdonnement
7. ruche
8. peut-être
9. effroyable
10. badine
11. quand il remettait quelque récalcitrant sur
12. riant chemin du savoir
13. « châtier peu c'est ne pas aimer assez ».
14. très aimés
15. ne voudrais pas qu'on s'imagine
16. se délectent de la souffrance
17. discernement
18. fardeau
19. Le gringalet qui grimaçait
20. menace
21. baguette
22. épargné
23. exigences
24. à tête dure et à larges basques
25. polisson
26. boudait
27. bouillait de rage
28. mais restait obstinément impassible
29. envers

so consolatory to the smarting urchin[1], that "he would remember it and thank him for it the longest day he had to live[2]."

When school hours were over, he was even the companion and playmate[3] of the larger boys; and on holiday afternoons would convoy[4] some of the smaller ones home, who happened to have pretty sisters, or good housewives for mothers, noted for the comforts of the cupboard[5]. Indeed, it behooved him[6] to keep on good terms with his pupils. The revenue arising from his school was small, and would have been scarcely sufficient to furnish him with daily bread, for he was a huge feeder[7], and, though lank, had the dilating powers of an anaconda; but to help out his maintenance[8], he was, according to country custom in those parts[9], boarded and lodged[10] at the houses of the farmers whose children he instructed. With these he lived successively a week at a time, thus going the rounds[11] of the neighborhood, with all his worldly effects[12] tied up in a cotton handkerchief.

That all this might not be[13] too onerous on the purses[14] of his rustic patrons[15], who are apt to[16] consider the costs of schooling a grievous[17] burden, and schoolmasters as mere drones[18], he had various ways of rendering himself both useful and agreeable. He assisted the farmers occasionally in the lighter labors of their farms, helped to make hay[19], mended the fences[20], took the horses to water[21], drove the cows from pasture, and cut wood for the winter fire. He laid aside, too, all the dominant dignity and absolute sway[22] with which he lorded it in[23] his little empire, the school, and became wonderfully gentle and ingratiating[24]. He

1. polisson rossé
2. jusqu'à la fin de ses jours
3. l'ami et compagnon de jeu
4. il escortait
5. réputées pour la richesse de leur garde-manger
6. il était de son intérêt
7. gros mangeur
8. l'aider à subsister
9. la région
10. logé et nourri
11. faisant le tour
12. biens personnels
13. Afin que tout cela ne fût pas
14. lourd pour la bourse
15. hôtes ruraux
16. ont tendance à
17. pénible
18. de simples parasites
19. les foins
20. réparait les clôtures
21. menait boire les chevaux
22. pouvoir
23. régnait sur
24. affable

found favor in the eyes of the[1] mothers by petting[2] the children, particularly the youngest; and like the lion bold, which whilom[3] so magnanimously the lamb did hold[4], he would sit with a child on one knee, and rock a cradle with his foot[5] for whole hours together.

In addition to his other vocations, he was the singing-master of the neighborhood, and picked up many bright shillings[6] by instructing the young folks in psalmody. It was a matter of no little vanity to him[7] on Sundays, to take his station[8] in front of the church gallery, with a band of chosen singers; where, in his own mind, he completely carried away[9] the palm from the parson[10]. Certain it is, his voice resounded far above all the rest of the congregation; and there are peculiar quavers[11] still to be heard in that church, and which may even be heard half a mile off, quite to the opposite side of the millpond[12], on a still[13] Sunday morning, which are said to be legitimately descended from the nose of Ichabod Crane. Thus, by divers little makeshifts[14], in that ingenious way which is commonly denominated "by hook and by crook[15]," the worthy[16] pedagogue got on tolerably enough[17], and was thought, by all who understood nothing of the labor of headwork[18], to have a wonderfully easy life of it.

The schoolmaster is generally a man of some importance in the female[19] circle of a rural neighborhood; being considered a kind of idle[20], gentlemanlike personage, of vastly superior taste and accomplishments to the rough country swains[21], and, indeed, inferior in learning[22] only to the parson. His appearance, therefore, is apt to occasion[23] some little stir[24] at the tea-table of a farm-

1. s'attirait les bonnes grâces des
2. choyant
3. jadis
4. tenait l'agneau [formule d'un vieil alphabet américain, à la lettre L : *The lion bold/The lamb doth hold*]
5. balançait du pied un berceau
6. récoltait un petit pactole
7. Il n'était pas peu fier,
8. place
9. ravissait
10. du pasteur
11. vibratos
12. bief du moulin
13. calme
14. expédients
15. par tous les moyens possibles et imaginables
16. digne
17. vivait plutôt bien
18. au travail cérébral
19. féminin
20. oisif
21. à ceux des frustes fermiers
22. en érudition
23. a donc tendance à provoquer
24. quelque agitation

house, and the addition of a supernumerary[1] dish of cakes or sweetmeats[2], or, peradventure[3], the parade of a silver teapot. Our man of letters, therefore, was peculiarly happy in the smiles of all the country damsels[4]. How he would figure among them in the churchyard, between services on Sundays; gathering grapes[5] for them from the wild vines that overran[6] the surrounding trees; reciting for their amusement all the epitaphs on the tombstones; or sauntering[7], with a whole bevy of them[8], along the banks[9] of the adjacent millpond; while the more bashful country bumpkins[10] hung sheepishly back[11], envying his superior elegance and address.

From his half-itinerant life, also, he was a kind of traveling gazette, carrying the whole budget[12] of local gossip[13] from house to house, so that his appearance was always greeted with satisfaction. He was, moreover, esteemed by the women as a man of great erudition, for he had read several books quite through[14], and was a perfect master of[15] Cotton Mather's "History of New England Witchcraft[16]," in which, by the way, he most firmly and potently believed.

He was, in fact, an odd mixture of small shrewdness[17] and simple credulity. His appetite for the marvellous, and his powers of[18] digesting it, were equally extraordinary; and both had been increased by his residence in this spellbound[19] region. No tale was too gross[20] or monstrous for his capacious swallow[21]. It was often his delight, after his school was dismissed[22] in the afternoon, to stretch himself on the rich bed of clover[23] bordering the little brook that whimpered[24] by his schoolhouse, and there con over[25]

1. supplémentaire
2. friandises
3. peut-être
4. jeunes filles
5. cueillant du raisin
6. envahissaient
7. flânant
8. essaim [de demoiselles]
9. berges
10. timides rustauds du coin
11. restaient, penauds, en arrière
12. la totalité
13. ragots
14. en entier
15. maîtrisait parfaitement
16. sorcellerie
17. mesquinerie
18. capacité à
19. envoûtée
20. énorme
21. pour qu'il la gobe
22. la fin de ses cours
23. trèfle
24. gazouillait
25. de lire et relire

old Mather's direful[1] tales, until the gathering dusk of evening[2] made the printed page a mere mist[3] before his eyes. Then, as he wended his way[4] by swamp[5] and stream and awful woodland, to the farmhouse where he happened to be quartered[6], every sound of nature, at that witching[7] hour, fluttered[8] his excited imagination,—the moan of the whip-poor-will[9] from the hillside, the boding[10] cry of the tree toad, that harbinger[11] of storm, the dreary hooting[12] of the screech owl[13], or the sudden rustling[14] in the thicket[15] of birds frightened from their roost[16]. The fireflies[17], too, which sparkled[18] most vividly in the darkest places, now and then startled him, as one of uncommon brightness[19] would stream across his path; and if, by chance[20], a huge blockhead[21] of a beetle came winging his blundering flight against him[22], the poor varlet[23] was ready to give up the ghost[24], with the idea that he was struck with a witch's token[25]. His only[26] resource on such occasions, either to drown thought[27] or drive away evil spirits[28], was to sing psalm tunes and the good people of Sleepy Hollow, as they sat by their doors of an evening, were often filled with awe[29] at hearing his nasal melody, "in linked sweetness long drawn out[30]," floating from the distant hill, or along the dusky[31] road.

Another of his sources of fearful pleasure was to pass long winter evenings with the old Dutch wives, as they sat spinning[32] by the fire, with a row of apples roasting and spluttering along the hearth[33], and listen to their marvellous tales of ghosts and goblins[34], and haunted fields, and haunted brooks, and haunted bridges, and haunt-

1. sinistres
2. crépuscule
3. ne brouille les pages
4. cheminait
5. les marais
6. logeait alors
7. magique
8. titillait
9. l'engoulevent
10. prophétique
11. annonceur
12. hululement
13. chouette effraie
14. bruissement
15. fourré
16. et quittant leur perchoir
17. lucioles
18. scintillaient
19. quand l'une particulièrement vive
20. hasard
21. imbécile
22. venait le cogner dans sa fuite
23. diable
24. rendre l'âme
25. marque
26. seule
27. noyer ses pensées
28. écarter les mauvais esprits
29. d'effroi
30. s'étirant joliment [vers tiré de *L'Allegro* de John Milton, 1645]
31. ténébreuse
32. filaient
33. foyer
34. de lutins

ed houses, and particularly of the headless horseman, or Galloping Hessian of the Hollow, as they sometimes called him. He would delight them equally by his anecdotes of witchcraft, and of the direful omens[1] and portentous sights and sounds in the air[2], which prevailed in the earlier times of Connecticut; and would frighten them woefully[3] with speculations upon comets and shooting stars; and with the alarming fact that the world did absolutely turn round, and that they were half the time topsy-turvy[4]!

But if there was a pleasure in all this, while snugly cuddling[5] in the chimney corner of a chamber[6] that was all of a ruddy glow[7] from the crackling wood fire, and where, of course, no spectre dared to show its face, it was dearly purchased[8] by the terrors of his subsequent walk homewards[9]. What fearful shapes and shadows beset his path[10], amidst the dim and ghastly glare of a snowy night! With what wistful look did he eye[11] every trembling ray of light streaming across the waste fields from some distant window! How often was he appalled[12] by some shrub[13] covered with snow, which, like a sheeted[14] spectre, beset his very path[15]! How often did he shrink with curdling awe[16] at the sound of his own steps on the frosty crust beneath his feet; and dread[17] to look over his shoulder, lest he should behold[18] some uncouth being[19] tramping[20] close behind him[21]! And how often was he thrown into complete dismay[22] by some rushing blast[23], howling among the trees, in the idea that it was the Galloping Hessian on one of his nightly scourings[24]!

All these, however, were mere terrors of the night, phantoms of the mind that walk in dark-

1. présages
2. apparitions et sons de mauvais augure
3. terriblement
4. la tête en bas
5. tandis qu'il était douillettement installé
6. pièce
7. rougeoyante
8. chèrement payé
9. retour au logis
10. l'assaillaient sur le chemin
11. quel air de regret il contemplait
12. épouvanté
13. buisson
14. recouvert d'un drap
15. chemin
16. il se glaçait
17. comme il redoutait
18. de crainte d'apercevoir
19. vile créature
20. marchant
21. sur ses talons
22. désarroi
23. rafale
24. chevauchées

ness; and though he had seen many spectres in his time, and been more than once beset by Satan in divers shapes, in his lonely perambulations, yet daylight put an end to all these evils; and he would have passed a pleasant life of it, in despite of the[1] Devil and all his works, if his path had not been crossed by a being that causes more perplexity to mortal man than ghosts, goblins, and the whole race of witches put together, and that was—a woman.

Among the musical disciples[2] who assembled, one evening in each week, to receive his instructions in psalmody, was Katrina Van Tassel, the daughter and only child[3] of a substantial[4] Dutch farmer. She was a blooming lass of fresh eighteen[5]; plump as a partridge[6]; ripe and melting[7] and rosy-cheeked[8] as one of her father's peaches, and universally famed, not merely for her beauty, but her vast expectations[9]. She was withal[10] a little of a coquette, as might be perceived even in her dress, which was a mixture of ancient and modern fashions, as most suited to set off[11] her charms. She wore the ornaments of pure yellow gold, which her great-great-grandmother had brought over from Saardam[12]; the tempting stomacher[13] of the olden time, and withal a provokingly short petticoat[14], to display the prettiest foot and ankle in the country round.

Ichabod Crane had a soft and foolish heart[15] towards the sex[16]; and it is not to be wondered at that so tempting a morsel[17] soon found favor in his eyes, more especially after he had visited her in her paternal mansion. Old Baltus Van Tassel was a perfect picture of a thriving[18], contented, liberal-hearted[19] farmer. He seldom[20], it

1. en dépit du
2. ses élèves en musique
3. fille unique
4. riche
5. fraîche jeune fille de tout juste 18 ans
6. dodue comme une perdrix
7. fondante
8. aux joues roses
9. espérances
10. en outre
11. et comme faits pour mettre en valeur
12. Zandaam [ville néerlandaise]
13. aguichant corsage brodé [*pièce d'estomac* ; partie d'une robe à la française]
14. jupon
15. inclination
16. beau sexe
17. l'on ne s'étonnera guère qu'un tel appât
18. prospère
19. généreux
20. rarement

is true, sent either his eyes or his thoughts beyond the boundaries of his own farm; but within those everything was snug[1], happy and well-conditioned[2]. He was satisfied with his wealth, but not proud of it; and piqued himself upon the hearty[3] abundance, rather than the style in which he lived. His stronghold[4] was situated on the banks of the Hudson, in one of those green, sheltered, fertile nooks in which the Dutch farmers are so fond of nestling[5]. A great elm tree[6] spread its broad branches over it, at the foot of which bubbled up a spring[7] of the softest and sweetest water, in a little well[8] formed of a barrel; and then stole sparkling away[9] through the grass, to a neighboring brook, that babbled along[10] among alders[11] and dwarf willows[12]. Hard by[13] the farmhouse was a vast barn, that might have served for a church; every window and crevice of which seemed bursting forth with the[14] treasures of the farm; the flail[15] was busily resounding within it from morning to night; swallows and martins[16] skimmed twittering about the eaves[17]; and rows of pigeons, some with one eye turned up, as if watching the weather, some with their heads under their wings or buried in their bosoms[18], and others swelling[19], and cooing[20], and bowing about their dames[21], were enjoying the sunshine on the roof. Sleek unwieldy porkers[22] were grunting in the repose and abundance of their pens[23], from whence sallied forth[24], now and then, troops of sucking pigs[25], as if to snuff[6] the air. A stately squadron of snowy geese[27] were riding in an adjoining pond, convoying whole fleets of ducks; regiments of turkeys were gobbling[28] through the farmyard, and Guinea fowls[29] fretting

1. propret
2. bien tenu
3. solide
4. domaine
5. aiment tant s'installer
6. orme
7. gargouillait une source
8. puits
9. avant d'aller se jeter en scintillant
10. continuait gaiement son chemin
11. les aulnes
12. saules nains
13. Tout près de
14. et dont le moindre recoin débordait des
15. fléau
16. des hirondelles et des martinets
17. rasaient les gouttières en piaillant
18. jabot
19. se gonflant
20. roucoulant
21. courtisant leurs femelles
22. De lourds gorets au poil lustré
23. enclos
24. d'où sortaient gaiement
25. cochons de lait
26. renifler
27. digne escadron d'oies blanches
28. glougloutaient
29. des pintades

about it, like ill-tempered[1] housewives, with their peevish[2], discontented cry. Before the barn door strutted[3] the gallant cock, that pattern of a husband[4], a warrior and a fine gentleman, clapping his burnished[5] wings and crowing in the[6] pride and gladness of his heart,—sometimes tearing up the earth with his feet, and then generously calling his ever-hungry family of wives and children to enjoy the rich morsel which he had discovered.

The pedagogue's mouth watered[7] as he looked upon this sumptuous promise of luxurious winter fare[8]. In his devouring mind's eye[9], he pictured to himself every roasting-pig running about with a pudding in his belly, and an apple in his mouth; the pigeons were snugly put to bed[10] in a comfortable pie, and tucked in with a coverlet[11] of crust; the geese were swimming in their own gravy[12]; and the ducks pairing[13] cosily in dishes, like snug married couples, with a decent competency[14] of onion sauce. In the porkers he saw carved out the future sleek side[15] of bacon, and juicy relishing[16] ham; not a turkey but he beheld daintily trussed up[17], with its gizzard[18] under its wing, and, peradventure, a necklace of savory sausages; and even bright chanticleer[19] himself lay sprawling[20] on his back, in a side dish, with uplifted claws[21], as if craving that quarter[22] which his chivalrous spirit disdained to ask while living.

As the enraptured Ichabod fancied[23] all this, and as he rolled his great green eyes over the fat meadow lands[24], the rich fields of wheat, of rye[25], of buckwheat[26], and Indian corn[27], and the orchards[28] burdened with ruddy[29] fruit, which surrounded the warm tenement[30] of Van Tassel, his heart yearned after[31] the damsel who was to

1. acariâtres
2. grincheux
3. se pavanait
4. mari modèle
5. brillantes
6. chantant de toute la
7. L'eau venait à la bouche de l'instituteur
8. festins
9. esprit affamé
10. douillettement étendus
11. bien bordés d'une couverture
12. sauce
13. s'appariaient
14. quantité raisonnable
15. voyait déjà la future tranche émincée
16. savoureux
17. qui ne lui apparût délicatement troussée
18. gésier
19. Chantecler
20. reposait
21. pattes en l'air
22. s'il demandait la grâce
23. Tandis que, ravi, Ichabod s'imaginait
24. grasses prairies
25. seigle
26. sarrasin
27. de maïs
28. vergers
29. dorés
30. demeure
31. soupirait pour

inherit these domains, and his imagination expanded with the idea, how they might be readily turned into cash[1], and the money invested in immense tracts[2] of wild land, and shingle palaces[3] in the wilderness. Nay[4], his busy fancy[5] already realized his hopes, and presented to him the blooming Katrina, with a whole family of children, mounted on the top of a wagon loaded with household trumpery[6], with pots and kettles[7] dangling beneath; and he beheld himself bestriding a pacing mare[8], with a colt[9] at her heels, setting out for[10] Kentucky, Tennessee,—or the Lord knows where!

When he entered the house, the conquest of his heart was complete. It was one of those spacious farmhouses, with high-ridged but lowly sloping[11] roofs, built in the style handed down from[12] the first Dutch settlers; the low projecting eaves[13] forming a piazza[14] along the front, capable of being closed up in bad weather. Under this were hung flails[15], harness, various utensils of husbandry[16], and nets for fishing in the neighboring river. Benches were built along the sides for summer use; and a great spinning-wheel[17] at one end, and a churn[18] at the other, showed the various uses to which this important porch might be devoted. From this piazza the wondering[19] Ichabod entered the hall, which formed the centre of the mansion, and the place of usual residence. Here rows of resplendent pewter[20], ranged on a long dresser[21], dazzled his eyes[22]. In one corner stood a huge bag of wool, ready to be spun; in another, a quantity of linsey-woolsey[23] just from the loom[24]; ears[25] of Indian corn, and strings of dried apples and peaches, hung in gay festoons along

1. facilement monnayés
2. étendues
3. somptueuses maisons en bois
4. Ou plutôt
5. imagination
6. d'ustensiles ménagers
7. des bouilloires
8. chevauchant une paisible jument
9. poulain
10. prenant la direction du
11. hauts et descendant très bas
12. transmis par
13. avant-toits en saillie
14. véranda
15. des fléaus [pour battre les grains]
16. agricoles
17. rouet
18. baratte
19. l'émerveillé
20. d'étains resplendissants
21. buffet
22. l'éblouirent
23. toile [en lin et laine]
24. métier à tisser
25. des épis

the walls, mingled with the gaud of red peppers[1]; and a door left ajar[2] gave him a peep into[3] the best parlor[4], where the claw-footed[5] chairs and dark mahogany[6] tables shone like mirrors; andirons[7], with their accompanying shovel and tongs[8], glistened from their covert of asparagus tops[9]; mock-oranges[10] and conch-shells[11] decorated the mantelpiece[12]; strings of various-colored birds eggs were suspended above it; a great ostrich egg was hung from the centre of the room, and a corner cupboard, knowingly[13] left open, displayed immense treasures of old silver and well-mended china[14].

From the moment Ichabod laid his eyes upon these regions of delight, the peace of his mind was at an end[15], and his only study was how to gain the affections of the peerless[16] daughter of Van Tassel. In this enterprise, however, he had more real difficulties than generally fell to the lot of a knight-errant of yore[17], who seldom had anything but[18] giants, enchanters, fiery dragons, and such like[19] easily conquered adversaries, to contend with[20] and had to make his way merely through gates of iron and brass[21], and walls of adamant[22] to the castle keep[23], where the lady of his heart was confined; all which he achieved as easily as a man would carve his way[24] to the centre of a Christmas pie; and then the lady gave him her hand as a matter of course[25]. Ichabod, on the contrary, had to win his way to[26] the heart of a country coquette, beset with a[27] labyrinth of whims[28] and caprices, which were forever presenting new difficulties and impediments[29]; and he had to encounter a host[30] of fearful adversaries of real flesh and blood, the numerous rustic ad-

1. au rouge vif des poivrons
2. entrebâillée
3. lui fit entrevoir
4. grand salon
5. à pieds griffus
6. en acajou
7. des chenets
8. pincettes
9. de dessous leurs motifs en pointes d'asperge
10. de fausses oranges
11. des coquillages
12. tablette de cheminée
13. délibérément
14. de porcelaine à peine ébréchée
15. disparut
16. incomparable
17. que n'en rencontrait le chevalier errant du temps jadis
18. avait rarement autre chose que
19. et autres
20. à affronter
21. de cuivre
22. roche dure
23. du donjon
24. pénétrerait
25. tout naturellement
26. conquérir
27. cerné d'un
28. fantaisies
29. obstacles
30. foule

mirers, who beset every portal to her heart, keeping a watchful and angry eye upon each other, but ready to fly out in the common cause[1] against any new competitor.

Among these, the most formidable[2] was a burly[3], roaring[4], roistering[5] blade[6], of the name of Abraham—or, according to the Dutch abbreviation, Brom—Van Brunt, the hero of the country round[7], which rang with his feats[8] of strength and hardihood. He was broad-shouldered and double-jointed[9], with short curly black hair, and a bluff[10] but not unpleasant countenance[11], having a mingled air of fun and arrogance. From his Herculean frame[12] and great powers of limb[13] he had received the nickname of BROM BONES, by which he was universally known. He was famed for great knowledge and skill in horsemanship[14], being as dexterous[15] on horseback as a Tartar. He was foremost[16] at all races and cock fights; and, with the ascendancy which bodily strength always acquires in rustic life, was the umpire[17] in all disputes, setting his hat on one side, and giving his decisions with an air and tone that admitted of no gainsay[18] or appeal. He was always ready for either a fight or a frolic[19]; but had more mischief[20] than ill-will[21] in his composition; and with all his overbearing roughness[22], there was a strong dash of waggish good[23] humor at bottom. He had three or four boon companions[24], who regarded him as their model, and at the head of whom he scoured[25] the country, attending every scene of feud[26] or merriment[27] for miles round. In cold weather he was distinguished by a fur cap, surmounted with a flaunting[28] fox's tail; and when the folks at a country gathering descried[29]

1. faire cause commune
2. redoutable
3. solide
4. bruyant
5. joyeux
6. gaillard
7. alentour
8. retentissait de ses exploits
9. large d'épaules et très souple
10. abrupte
11. expression
12. carrure
13. musculature
14. expertise de cavalier
15. agile
16. le premier
17. arbitre
18. contradiction
19. espièglerie
20. de malice
21. de méchanceté
22. malgré sa grande rudesse
23. badine
24. joyeux compères
25. arpentait
26. se rendant à tout lieu de dissension
27. de festivités
28. glorieuse
29. apercevaient

this well-known crest at a distance, whisking about[1] among a squad of hard riders, they always stood by for a squall[2]. Sometimes his crew[3] would be heard dashing along past the farmhouses at midnight, with whoop and halloo[4], like a troop of Don Cossacks[5]; and the old dames, startled out of their sleep, would listen for a moment till the hurry-scurry had clattered by[6], and then exclaim, "Ay, there goes Brom Bones and his gang!" The neighbors looked upon him with a mixture of awe, admiration, and good-will; and, when any madcap prank[7] or rustic brawl[8] occurred in the vicinity, always shook their heads, and warranted[9] Brom Bones was at the bottom of it.

This rantipole[10] hero had for some time singled out[11] the blooming Katrina for the object of his uncouth[12] gallantries, and though his amorous toyings[13] were something like the gentle caresses and endearments[14] of a bear, yet it was whispered that she did not altogether[15] discourage his hopes. Certain it is, his advances were signals for rival candidates to retire, who felt no inclination to cross[16] a lion in his amours; insomuch,[17] that when his horse was seen tied to Van Tassel's paling[18], on a Sunday night, a sure sign that his master was courting, or, as it is termed, "sparking[19]," within, all other suitors passed by in despair, and carried the war into other quarters.

Such was the formidable rival with whom Ichabod Crane had to contend[20], and, considering all things, a stouter[21] man than he would have shrunk[22] from the competition, and a wiser man would have despaired. He had, however, a happy mixture of pliability[23] and perseverance in his nature; he was in form and spirit like a

1. s'agitant
2. étaient toujours prêts à l'acclamer
3. bande
4. des cris de triomphe
5. cosaques du Don [sud de la Russie]
6. jusqu'à ce que la bruyante cavalcade fût passée
7. quelque bouffonnerie
8. bagarre
9. gageaient que
10. tapageur
11. choisi
12. frustes
13. cajoleries
14. la tendresse
15. complètement
16. contrarier
17. à tel point
18. palissade
19. flirtait
20. affaire
21. plus vaillant
22. se serait retiré
23. docilité

supple-jack[1]—yielding, but tough[2]; though he bent, he never broke; and though he bowed beneath the slightest pressure, yet, the moment[3] it was away—jerk![4]—he was as erect[5], and carried his head as high as ever.

To have taken the field[6] openly against his rival would have been madness; for he was not a man to be thwarted[7] in his amours, any more than that stormy lover, Achilles. Ichabod, therefore[8], made his advances in a quiet and gently insinuating manner. Under cover of his character[9] of singing-master, he made frequent visits at the farmhouse; not that he had anything to apprehend from the meddlesome interference of parents[10], which is so often a stumbling-block[11] in the path of lovers. Balt Van Tassel was an easy indulgent soul[12]; he loved his daughter better even than his pipe, and, like a reasonable man and an excellent father, let her have her way[13] in everything. His notable little wife, too, had enough to do to attend to her housekeeping and manage her poultry[14]; for, as she sagely observed, ducks and geese are foolish things, and must be looked after, but girls can take care of themselves. Thus, while the busy dame bustled about[15] the house, or plied[16] her spinning-wheel at one end of the piazza, honest Balt would sit smoking his evening pipe at the other, watching the achievements[17] of a little wooden warrior, who, armed with a sword in each hand, was most valiantly fighting the wind on the pinnacle of the barn. In the mean time[18], Ichabod would carry on his suit with[19] the daughter by the side of the spring under the great elm, or sauntering along[20] in the twilight, that hour so favorable to the lover's eloquence.

1. tel le roseau
2. souple mais résistant
3. dès que
4. hop !
5. droit
6. Entrer en campagne
7. contrarié
8. par conséquent
9. qualité
10. que les parents s'interposent
11. obstacle
12. personne
13. agir à sa guise
14. la volaille
15. s'affairait dans
16. maniait
17. exploits
18. Pendant ce temps
19. faisait sa cour à
20. l'emmenait se promener

I profess not[1] to know how women's hearts are wooed[2] and won. To me they have always been matters of riddle[3] and admiration. Some seem to have but one[4] vulnerable point, or door of access; while others have a thousand avenues[5], and may be captured in a thousand different ways. It is a great triumph of skill to gain the former[6], but a still greater proof of generalship[7] to maintain possession of the latter, for[8] man must battle for his fortress at every door and window. He[9] who wins a thousand common hearts is therefore entitled to some renown; but he who keeps undisputed sway[10] over the heart of a coquette is indeed a hero. Certain it is, this was not the case with the redoubtable Brom Bones; and from the moment Ichabod Crane made his advances, the interests of the former evidently declined: his horse was no longer seen tied to the palings on Sunday nights, and a deadly feud gradually arose[11] between him and the preceptor of Sleepy Hollow.

Brom, who had a degree of rough chivalry[12] in his nature, would fain have carried matters to open warfare[13] and have settled their pretensions to the lady, according to the mode of those most concise and simple reasoners, the knights-errant of yore,—by single combat[14]; but Ichabod was too conscious of the superior might[15] of his adversary to enter the lists[16] against him; he had overheard a boast of Bones, that he would[17] "double the schoolmaster up[18], and lay him on a shelf of his own schoolhouse;" and he was too wary[19] to give him an opportunity. There was something extremely provoking in this obstinately pacific system; it left Brom no alternative but to draw upon the funds of rustic waggery in his disposition[20],

1. ne prétends pas
2. courtisés
3. énigme
4. un seul
5. biais
6. conquérir les premières
7. de qualités de stratège
8. car
9. Celui
10. son emprise exclusive sur
11. terrible mésentente se fit jour
12. certaine brutalité chevaleresque
13. aurait volontiers appelé aux armes
14. en combat singulier
15. force
16. entrer en lice
17. entendu Bones prétendre qu'il
18. plierait en deux le maître d'école
19. méfiant
20. d'autre solution que de puiser dans son fonds naturel de facéties rustiques

and to play off boorish practical jokes upon[1] his rival. Ichabod became the object of whimsical[2] persecution to Bones and his gang of rough riders. They harried[3] his hitherto[4] peaceful domains; smoked out[5] his singing school by stopping up[6] the chimney; broke[7] into the schoolhouse at night, in spite of its formidable fastenings of withe and window stakes[8], and turned everything topsy-turvy[9], so that the poor schoolmaster began to think all the witches in the country held their meetings there. But what was still more annoying, Brom took all opportunities of turning him into ridicule in presence of his mistress[10], and had a scoundrel[11] dog whom he taught to whine[12] in the most ludicrous[13] manner, and introduced as a rival of Ichabod's, to instruct her in psalmody[14].

In this way matters went on for some time, without producing any material[15] effect on the relative situations of the contending powers[16]. On a fine autumnal afternoon, Ichabod, in pensive mood, sat enthroned[17] on the lofty stool[18] from whence[19] he usually watched all the concerns of his little literary realm. In his hand he swayed[20] a ferule, that sceptre of despotic power; the birch[21] of justice reposed on three nails behind the throne, a constant terror to evil doers[22], while on the desk before him might be seen sundry[23] contraband articles and prohibited weapons, detected upon the persons of idle urchins[24], such as half-munched[25] apples, popguns[26], whirligigs[27], fly-cages[28], and whole legions of rampant little paper gamecocks[29]. Apparently there had been some appalling act of justice recently inflicted, for his scholars[30] were all busily intent upon[31] their books, or slyly[32] whispering behind them

1. jouer de très mauvais tours à
2. fantaisiste
3. harcelaient
4. jusque-là
5. enfumaient
6. en bouchant
7. entraient par effraction
8. énormes attaches sur les volets
9. sens dessus dessous
10. dulcinée
11. misérable
12. glapir
13. ridicule
14. pour lui donner des cours de chant
15. notable
16. rivaux
17. trônait
18. haut tabouret
19. d'où
20. agitait
21. bâton
22. sacripants
23. divers
24. garnements désœuvrés
25. à demi croquées
26. des pétoires
27. moulins à vent
28. cages à mouches
29. cocottes en papier
30. élèves
31. penchés sur
32. sournoisement

with one eye kept upon the master; and a kind of buzzing stillness reigned throughout the school-room. It was suddenly interrupted by the appearance of a negro in tow-cloth[1] jacket and trowsers, a round-crowned fragment of a hat[2], like the cap of Mercury, and mounted on the back of a ragged[3], wild, half-broken[4] colt[5], which he managed with a rope by way of halter[6]. He came clattering up[7] to the school door with an invitation to Ichabod to attend a merry-making[8] or "quilting frolic[9]," to be held that evening at Mynheer[10] Van Tassel's; and having delivered his message with that air of importance, and effort at fine language, which a negro is apt to display on petty embassies[11] of the kind, he dashed over the brook, and was seen scampering away up[12] the hollow, full of the importance and hurry of his mission.

All was now bustle and hubbub[13] in the late quiet schoolroom. The scholars were hurried through their lessons without stopping at trifles[14]; those who were nimble[15] skipped over[16] half with impunity, and those who were tardy[17] had a smart application[18] now and then in the rear[19], to quicken their speed or help them[20] over a tall[21] word. Books were flung aside without being put away on the shelves, inkstands[22] were overturned, benches thrown down, and the whole school was turned loose[23] an hour before the usual time, bursting forth like a legion of young imps[24], yelping and racketing[25] about the green[26] in joy at their early emancipation[27].

The gallant Ichabod now spent at least an extra[28] half hour at his toilet, brushing and furbishing up[29] his best, and indeed only suit of rusty black[30], and arranging his locks[31] by[32] a bit of

1. de filasse
2. sorte de restes d'un chapeau en couronne
3. hirsute
4. encore mal dressé
5. poulain
6. en guise de licou
7. arriva bruyamment
8. assister à un divertissement
9. une soirée Rires et couture
10. chez Monsieur
11. de petites missions
12. on le vit remonter à toute allure
13. Ce fut alors un tohu-bohu
14. aux détails
15. agiles
16. en sautèrent
17. plus lents
18. reçurent l'encouragement d'un coup de badine
19. dans le dos
20. de se faire aider
21. difficile
22. les encriers
23. libérée
24. diablotins
25. tout criaillant
26. sur l'herbe
27. d'être libres plus tôt
28. de plus
29. astiquant
30. brun-noir
31. boucles de cheveux
32. devant

broken looking-glass that hung up in the school-house. That he might[1] make his appearance before his mistress in the true style of a cavalier, he borrowed a horse from the farmer with whom he was domiciliated, a choleric old Dutchman of the name of Hans Van Ripper, and, thus gallantly mounted, issued forth[2] like a knight-errant in quest of adventures. But it is meet I should[3], in the true spirit of romantic story, give some account[4] of the looks and equipments of my hero and his steed[5]. The animal he bestrode[6] was a broken-down plow-horse[7], that had outlived almost everything but[8] its viciousness. He was gaunt[9] and shagged[10], with a ewe neck[11], and a head like a hammer; his rusty mane and tail were tangled and knotted with burs[12]; one eye had lost its pupil, and was glaring and spectral, but the other had the gleam of a genuine devil[13] in it. Still he must have had fire and mettle[14] in his day, if we may judge from the name he bore of Gunpowder. He had, in fact, been a favorite steed[15] of his master's, the choleric Van Ripper, who was a furious rider, and had infused, very probably, some of his own spirit into the animal; for, old and broken-down as he looked, there was more of the lurking devil[16] in him than in any young filly[17] in the country.

Ichabod was a suitable figure for such a steed. He rode with short stirrups[18], which brought his knees nearly up to the pommel of the saddle[19]; his sharp elbows stuck out like grasshoppers'[20]; he carried his whip[21] perpendicularly in his hand, like a sceptre, and as his horse jogged on[22], the motion of his arms was not unlike the flapping of a pair of wings. A small wool hat rested on the

1. Afin de
2. s'élança
3. il serait juste que je
4. description
5. monture
6. montait
7. cheval de trait fourbu
8. à qui il ne restait pratiquement plus que
9. efflanqué
10. le poil peu soigné
11. encolure de cerf [trop arrondie]
12. des touffes de bardane [dont les capitules s'accrochent aux toisons] constellaient sa crinière et sa queue rousses
13. vrai diable
14. de la fougue
15. coursier
16. de trace de diable
17. pouliche
18. étriers
19. pommeau de la selle
20. ceux d'une sauterelle
21. cravache
22. allait cahin-caha

top of his nose, for so his scanty strip of forehead might be called[1], and the skirts[2] of his black coat fluttered out almost to the horse's tail. Such was the appearance of Ichabod and his steed as they shambled out of the gate[3] of Hans Van Ripper, and it was altogether such an apparition as is seldom to be met with[4] in broad daylight.

It was, as I have said, a fine autumnal day; the sky was clear and serene, and nature wore that rich and golden livery[5] which we always associate with the idea of abundance. The forests had put on their sober brown and yellow, while some trees of the tenderer kind had been nipped by the frosts into brilliant dyes of[6] orange, purple, and scarlet. Streaming files of wild ducks began to make their appearance high in the air; the bark[7] of the squirrel might be heard from the groves of beech and hickory-nuts[8], and the pensive whistle of the quail[9] at intervals from the neighboring stubble[10] field.

The small birds were taking their farewell banquets[11]. In the fullness[12] of their revelry[13], they fluttered, chirping and frolicking from bush to bush, and tree to tree, capricious from the very profusion and variety around them. There was the honest cock robin[14], the favorite game[15] of stripling sportsmen[16], with its loud querulous note; and the twittering blackbirds[17] flying in sable clouds[18]; and the golden-winged woodpecker with his crimson crest[19], his broad black gorget, and splendid plumage; and the cedar bird[20], with its red-tipt wings[21] and yellow-tipt tail and its little monteiro cap of feathers[22]; and the blue jay, that noisy coxcomb[23], in his gay light blue coat and white underclothes, screaming and chat-

1. si l'on pouvait ainsi nommer son front fuyant
2. basques
3. passaient d'un pas lourd la porte
4. un spectacle comme on en voit rarement
5. livrée
6. pris, sous les assauts du gel, de belles teintes
7. cri
8. forêts de hêtres et de noyers
9. caille
10. chaume
11. festin d'adieu
12. l'abondance
13. festivités
14. grive [merle d'Amérique]
15. gibier
16. jeunes chasseurs
17. merles
18. nuées noires
19. crête cramoisie
20. jaseur
21. ailes bordées de rouge
22. huppe
23. bellâtre

tering, nodding and bobbing and bowing[1], and pretending to be on good terms with every songster[2] of the grove.

As Ichabod jogged[3] slowly on his way, his eye, ever open to every symptom of culinary abundance, ranged with delight over the[4] treasures of jolly autumn. On all sides he beheld[5] vast store of apples; some hanging in oppressive opulence on the trees; some gathered into baskets and barrels for the market; others heaped up[6] in rich piles for the cider-press. Farther on he beheld great fields of Indian corn[7], with its golden ears[8] peeping from their leafy coverts[9], and holding out the promise of cakes and hasty-pudding[10]; and the yellow pumpkins lying beneath them, turning up their fair round bellies[11] to the sun, and giving ample prospects[12] of the most luxurious of pies; and anon[13] he passed the fragrant buckwheat fields breathing the odor of the beehive, and as he beheld them, soft anticipations stole over his mind of dainty slapjacks[14], well buttered, and garnished with honey or treacle[15], by the delicate little dimpled[16] hand of Katrina Van Tassel.

Thus feeding his mind with many sweet thoughts and "sugared suppositions," he journeyed along the sides of a range[17] of hills which look out upon some of the goodliest scenes of the mighty Hudson. The sun gradually wheeled his broad disk down[18] in the west. The wide bosom of the Tappan Zee lay motionless and glassy[19], excepting that here and there a gentle undulation waved and prolonged the blue shadow of the distant mountain. A few amber clouds floated in the sky, without a breath of air to move them. The horizon was of a fine golden tint, changing

1. remuant la tête en tous sens
2. chanteur
3. trottinait
4. se délectait des
5. voyait
6. entassées
7. maïs
8. épis
9. écrin feuillu
10. bouillies
11. jolie panse ronde
12. perspectives
13. bientôt
14. délicates galettes
15. de mélasse
16. potelée
17. chaîne
18. grand disque solaire s'abaissait
19. lisse comme un miroir

gradually into a pure apple green, and from that into the deep blue of the mid-heaven[1]. A slanting[2] ray lingered[3] on the woody crests of the precipices that overhung[4] some parts of the river, giving greater depth to the dark gray and purple of their rocky sides. A sloop[5] was loitering in the distance, dropping slowly down with the tide[6], her sail hanging uselessly against the mast; and as the reflection of the sky gleamed along the still water, it seemed as if the vessel[7] was suspended in the air.

It was toward evening that Ichabod arrived at the castle of the Heer Van Tassel, which he found thronged[8] with the pride and flower[9] of the adjacent country. Old farmers, a spare leathern-faced race[10], in homespun[11] coats and breeches[12], blue stockings[13], huge shoes, and magnificent pewter buckles[14]. Their brisk[15], withered[16] little dames, in close-crimped caps[17], long-waisted short gowns[18], homespun petticoats[19], with scissors and pincushions[20], and gay calico pockets hanging on the outside. Buxom lasses[21], almost as antiquated as their mothers, excepting where a straw hat, a fine ribbon, or perhaps a white frock[22], gave symptoms of city innovation. The sons, in short square-skirted coats, with rows of stupendous brass buttons, and their hair generally queued[23] in the fashion of the times, especially if they could procure an eel-skin[24] for the purpose, it[25] being esteemed throughout the country as a potent nourisher and strengthener of the hair.

Brom Bones, however, was the hero of the scene, having come to the gathering on his favorite steed Daredevil[26], a creature[27], like himself, full of mettle[28] and mischief[29], and which no

1. cieux
2. oblique
3. s'attardait
4. surplombaient
5. [petit voilier]
6. marée
7. bateau
8. rempli
9. fine fleur
10. secs et aux visages tannés
11. tissés à la main
12. culottes [pantalons]
13. bas
14. boucles [de ceinture]
15. très alertes
16. ridées
17. bonnets à fronces
18. robes
19. jupons
20. des pelotes à épingles
21. Des jeunes filles plantureuses
22. robe
23. attachés
24. avaient pu se procurer une peau d'anguille
25. celle-ci
26. Casse-cou
27. un être
28. fougue
29. malice

one but[1] himself could manage[2]. He was, in fact, noted for preferring vicious animals, given[3] to all kinds of tricks[4] which kept the rider in constant risk of his neck, for he held a tractable[5], well-broken[6] horse as unworthy[7] of a lad of spirit[8].

Fain would I pause to dwell[9] upon the world of charms that burst upon the enraptured gaze[10] of my hero, as he entered the state parlor[11] of Van Tassel's mansion. Not those of the bevy[12] of buxom lasses, with their luxurious display of red and white; but the ample charms of a genuine Dutch country tea-table, in the sumptuous time of autumn. Such heaped up platters[13] of cakes of various and almost indescribable kinds, known only to experienced Dutch housewives! There was the doughty doughnut[14], the tender oly koek, and the crisp and crumbling cruller[15]; sweet cakes and short cakes[16], ginger cakes and honey cakes, and the whole family of cakes. And then there were apple pies, and peach pies, and pumpkin pies; besides slices of ham and smoked beef; and moreover delectable dishes of preserved[17] plums, and peaches, and pears, and quinces[18]; not to mention broiled shad[19] and roasted chickens; together with bowls of milk and cream, all mingled higgledy-piggledy[20], pretty much as I have enumerated them, with the motherly teapot sending up its clouds of vapor from the midst—Heaven bless the mark[21]! I want breath and time[22] to discuss this banquet as it deserves, and am too eager[23] to get on with my story. Happily, Ichabod Crane was not in so great a hurry as his historian, but did ample justice to every dainty[24].

He was a kind and thankful creature, whose heart dilated in proportion as his skin was filled

1. à part
2. maîtriser
3. enclins
4. tours
5. docile
6. bien dressé
7. pour indigne
8. jeune homme de caractère
9. Je m'attarderais volontiers
10. se présenta au regard émerveillé
11. salle d'apparat
12. l'essaim
13. Des pyramides
14. bon beignet
15. [autres sortes de beignets]
16. des sablés
17. en conserve
18. des coings
19. de l'alose grillée [sorte de hareng]
20. disposés pêle-mêle
21. Dieu soit loué
22. n'ai ni le souffle ni le temps
23. pressé
24. gourmandise

with good cheer[1], and whose spirits rose[2] with eating, as some men's do with drink. He could not help[3], too, rolling his large eyes round him as he ate, and chuckling with the possibility[4] that he might one day be lord of all this scene of almost unimaginable luxury and splendor. Then, he thought, how soon he'd turn his back upon the[5] old schoolhouse; snap his[6] fingers in the face of Hans Van Ripper, and every other niggardly patron[7], and kick any itinerant pedagogue out of doors that should dare to call him comrade!

Old Baltus Van Tassel moved about[8] among his guests with a face dilated with content and good humor, round and jolly[9] as the harvest[10] moon. His hospitable attentions were brief, but expressive, being confined to a shake of the hand, a slap on the shoulder, a loud laugh, and a pressing invitation to "fall to, and help themselves[11]."

And now the sound of the music from the common room, or hall, summoned[12] to the dance. The musician was an old gray-headed negro, who had been the itinerant orchestra of the neighborhood for more than half a century. His instrument was as old and battered[13] as himself. The greater part of the time he scraped on[14] two or three strings, accompanying every movement of the bow[15] with a motion of the head; bowing[16] almost to the ground, and stamping with his foot[17] whenever a fresh[18] couple were to start.

Ichabod prided himself upon his dancing[19] as much as upon his vocal powers. Not a limb, not a fibre about him was idle; and to have seen his loosely hung frame[20] in full motion, and clattering about the room, you would have thought St. Vitus himself, that blessed patron of the dance,

1. chère
2. l'entrain s'accroît
3. s'empêcher de
4. glousser à l'idée
5. comme il se détournerait vite de la
6. claquerait des
7. avare logeur
8. circulait
9. jovial
10. pleine
11. foncer et se servir
12. donna le signal
13. abîmé
14. grattait
15. l'archet
16. s'inclinant
17. frappant du pied
18. nouveau
19. s'enorgueillissait de ses talents de danseur
20. corps dégingandé

was figuring before you in person. He was the admiration of all the negroes; who, having gathered, of all ages and sizes, from the farm and the neighborhood, stood forming a pyramid of shining black faces at every door and window, gazing with delight at the scene, rolling their white eyeballs, and showing grinning[1] rows of ivory from ear to ear. How could the flogger of urchins[2] be otherwise than animated and joyous? The lady of his heart was his partner in the dance, and smiling graciously in reply to all his amorous oglings[3]; while Brom Bones, sorely smitten with[4] love and jealousy, sat brooding by himself[5] in one corner.

When the dance was at an end, Ichabod was attracted to a knot[6] of the sager folks, who, with Old Van Tassel, sat smoking at one end of the piazza, gossiping over former times[7], and drawing out[8] long stories about the war.

This neighborhood[9], at the time of which I am speaking, was one of those highly favored places which abound with chronicle and great men. The British and American line[10] had run near it[11] during the war; it had, therefore[12], been the scene of marauding and infested with refugees, cowboys, and all kinds of border chivalry[13]. Just sufficient time had elapsed to enable each storyteller to dress up[14] his tale with a little becoming[15] fiction, and, in the indistinctness of his recollection[16], to make himself the hero of every exploit.

There was the story of Doffue Martling, a large blue-bearded Dutchman, who had nearly taken a British frigate[17] with an old iron nine-pounder[18] from a mud breastwork[19], only that his gun burst[20] at the sixth discharge[21]. And there was an old gentleman who shall be nameless[22], being too

1. de souriantes
2. fouetteur de garnements
3. œillades
4. déchiré par
5. ruminait tout seul
6. groupe
7. parlant du bon vieux temps
8. racontant
9. région
10. front entre Britanniques et Américains
11. passait tout près
12. par conséquent
13. chevalerie de frontière
14. enjoliver
15. plaisante
16. souvenirs
17. frégate
18. canon [tirant des boulets de 9 livres]
19. parapet en terre
20. si son arme n'avait explosé
21. tir
22. dont nous tairons le nom

rich a mynheer[1] to be lightly[2] mentioned, who, in the battle of White Plains, being an excellent master of defence, parried a musket-ball[3] with a small sword, insomuch[4] that he absolutely felt it whiz[5] round the blade, and glance off at the hilt[6]; in proof of which he was ready at any time to show the sword, with the hilt a little bent. There were several more that had been equally great in the field, not one of whom but was[7] persuaded that he had a considerable hand[8] in bringing the war to a happy termination.

But all these were nothing to the[9] tales of ghosts and apparitions that succeeded. The neighborhood is rich in legendary treasures of the kind. Local tales and superstitions thrive best in these sheltered, long-settled retreats; but are trampled under foot[10] by the shifting throng[11] that forms the population of most of our country places. Besides, there is no encouragement for ghosts in most of our villages, for they have scarcely had time to finish their first nap[12] and turn themselves in their graves[13], before their surviving friends have travelled away from the neighborhood; so that when they turn out[14] at night to walk their rounds, they have no acquaintance left to call upon[15]. This is perhaps the reason why we so seldom hear of ghosts except in our long-established Dutch communities.

The immediate cause, however, of the prevalence[16] of supernatural stories in these parts[17], was doubtless owing[18] to the vicinity of Sleepy Hollow. There was a contagion in the very air that blew from that haunted region; it breathed forth[19] an atmosphere of dreams and fancies infecting all the land. Several of the Sleepy Hollow people

1. monsieur trop riche
2. à la légère
3. para une balle de mousquet
4. au point
5. l'avait sentie siffler
6. ricocher sur la poignée
7. dont pas un seul qui ne fût
8. influence
9. en comparaison des
10. foulées aux pieds
11. foule changeante
12. somme
13. tombe
14. sortent
15. il ne leur reste aucune connaissance à qui rendre visite
16. fréquence
17. contrées
18. due
19. il en émanait

were present at Van Tassel's, and, as usual, were doling out[1] their wild and wonderful legends. Many dismal[2] tales were told about funeral trains, and mourning cries and wailings[3] heard and seen about the great tree where the unfortunate Major André was taken, and which stood in the neighborhood. Some mention was made also of the woman in white, that haunted the dark glen at Raven Rock, and was often heard to shriek[4] on winter nights before a storm, having perished there in the snow. The chief part[5] of the stories, however, turned upon the[6] favorite spectre of Sleepy Hollow, the Headless Horseman, who had been heard several times of late[7], patrolling the country; and, it was said, tethered[8] his horse nightly[9] among the graves in the churchyard.

The sequestered[10] situation of this church seems always to have made it a favorite haunt[11] of troubled spirits. It stands on a knoll[12], surrounded by locust-trees[13] and lofty elms[14], from among which its decent, whitewashed[15] walls shine modestly forth, like Christian purity beaming through the shades of retirement[16]. A gentle slope descends from it to a silver sheet of water, bordered by high trees, between which, peeps may be caught at[17] the blue hills of the Hudson. To look upon its grass-grown yard[18], where the sunbeams seem to sleep so quietly, one would think that there at least the dead might rest in peace. On one side of the church extends a wide woody dell[19], along which raves[20] a large brook[21] among broken rocks and trunks of fallen trees. Over a deep black part of the stream, not far from the church, was formerly thrown a wooden bridge; the road that led to it, and the bridge itself, were

1. narraient
2. lugubres
3. des cris et gémissements de deuil
4. qu'on entendait souvent hurler
5. L'essentiel
6. avait trait au
7. récemment
8. attachait
9. nuitamment
10. très retirée
11. repaire
12. tertre
13. des caroubiers
14. de nobles ormes
15. blanchis à la chaux
16. la solitude
17. on peut entrapercevoir
18. cimetière envahi par l'herbe
19. vallon boisé
20. court
21. ruisseau

1. en surplomb
2. l'assombrissaient
3. On raconta l'histoire
4. incursion
5. monter
6. fourrés
7. marais
8. s'était transformé en squelette
9. s'enfuit d'un bond
10. dans un coup
11. trois fois plus
12. traita
13. de lamentable cavalier
14. rattrapé
15. cheval fantôme
16. à plate couture
17. avait déguerpi
18. disparu
19. de cette voix basse et traînante
20. visage
21. de temps à autre la lueur
22. s'ancrèrent
23. leur rendit la pareille

thickly shaded by overhanging[1] trees, which cast a gloom about it[2], even in the daytime; but occasioned a fearful darkness at night. Such was one of the favorite haunts of the Headless Horseman, and the place where he was most frequently encountered. The tale was told[3] of old Brouwer, a most heretical disbeliever in ghosts, how he met the Horseman returning from his foray[4] into Sleepy Hollow, and was obliged to get up[5] behind him; how they galloped over bush and brake[6], over hill and swamp[7], until they reached the bridge; when the Horseman suddenly turned into a skeleton[8], threw old Brouwer into the brook, and sprang away[9] over the tree-tops with a clap[10] of thunder.

This story was immediately matched by a thrice[11] marvellous adventure of Brom Bones, who made light of[12] the Galloping Hessian as an arrant jockey[13]. He affirmed that on returning one night from the neighboring village of Sing Sing, he had been overtaken[14] by this midnight trooper; that he had offered to race with him for a bowl of punch, and should have won it too, for Daredevil beat the goblin horse[15] all hollow[16], but just as they came to the church bridge, the Hessian bolted[17], and vanished[18] in a flash of fire.

All these tales, told in that drowsy undertone[19] with which men talk in the dark, the countenances[20] of the listeners only now and then receiving a casual gleam[21] from the glare of a pipe, sank deep[22] in the mind of Ichabod. He repaid them in kind[23] with large extracts from his invaluable author, Cotton Mather, and added many marvellous events that had taken place in his native State of

Connecticut, and fearful sights which he had seen in his nightly walks about Sleepy Hollow.

The revel now gradually broke up[1]. The old farmers gathered together their families in their wagons, and were heard for some time rattling[2] along the hollow roads, and over the distant hills. Some of the damsels mounted on pillions behind their favorite swains[3], and their light-hearted laughter, mingling with the clatter of hoofs[4], echoed along the silent woodlands, sounding fainter and fainter, until they gradually died away,—and the late scene of noise and frolic was all silent and deserted. Ichabod only[5] lingered[6] behind, according to the custom of country lovers, to have a tête-à-tête with the heiress[7]; fully convinced that he was now on the high road to success. What passed at this interview I will not pretend to say, for in fact I do not know. Something, however, I fear me[8], must have gone wrong, for he certainly sallied forth[9], after no very great interval, with an air quite desolate and chapfallen[10]. Oh, these women! these women! Could that girl have been playing off any of her coquettish tricks? Was her encouragement of the poor pedagogue all a mere sham[11] to secure her conquest of his rival? Heaven only knows, not I! Let it suffice to say, Ichabod stole forth[12] with the air of one who had been sacking a henroost[13], rather than a fair lady's heart. Without looking to the right or left to notice the scene of rural wealth, on which he had so often gloated[14], he went straight to the stable[15], and with several hearty cuffs and kicks[16] roused his steed most uncourteously from the comfortable quarters in which he was sound-

1. La fête se disloquait peu à peu
2. brinquebalant
3. en croupe derrière leur soupirant
4. sabots
5. seul
6. resta
7. l'héritière
8. je le crains
9. sortit rapidement
10. fort affligé
11. qu'une comédie
12. s'échappa furtivement
13. aurait ravagé un poulailler
14. qu'il avait si souvent admirée
15. l'écurie
16. coups de pied et de main

ly sleeping, dreaming of mountains of corn and oats[1], and whole valleys of timothy and clover[2].

It was the very witching time[3] of night that[4] Ichabod, heavy-hearted and crestfallen[5], pursued his travels homewards[6], along the sides of the lofty hills which rise above Tarry Town, and which he had traversed so cheerily in the afternoon. The hour was as dismal[7] as himself. Far below him the Tappan Zee spread its dusky and indistinct waste[8] of waters, with here and there the tall mast of a sloop[9], riding quietly at anchor under the land. In the dead hush[10] of midnight, he could even hear the barking of the watchdog from the opposite shore of the Hudson; but it was so vague and faint[11] as only to give an idea of his distance from this faithful companion of man. Now and then, too, the long-drawn crowing[12] of a cock, accidentally awakened, would sound far, far off, from some farmhouse away among the hills—but it was like a dreaming sound in his ear. No signs of life occurred near him, but occasionally the melancholy chirp[13] of a cricket[14], or perhaps the guttural twang[15] of a bullfrog[16] from a neighboring marsh, as if sleeping uncomfortably and turning suddenly in his bed.

All the stories of ghosts and goblins that he had heard in the afternoon now came crowding upon his recollection[17]. The night grew darker and darker; the stars seemed to sink[18] deeper in the sky, and driving clouds occasionally hid them from his sight. He had never felt so lonely and dismal. He was, moreover, approaching the very place[19] where many of the scenes of the ghost stories had been laid[20]. In the centre of the road stood an enormous tulip-tree[21], which towered

1. d'avoine
2. fourrage et de trèfle
3. heure maléfique
4. où
5. très abattu
6. rentrait chez lui
7. sinistre
8. étendues
9. [petit voilier]
10. silence
11. ténu
12. long cocorico
13. grésillement mélancolique
14. grillon
15. grognement nasillard
16. grenouille
17. lui revinrent en mémoire
18. s'enfoncer
19. l'endroit exact
20. s'étaient déroulées
21. tulipier

like a giant above all the other trees of the neighborhood, and formed a kind of landmark[1]. Its limbs[2] were gnarled[3] and fantastic, large enough to form trunks for ordinary trees, twisting down almost to the earth, and rising again into the air. It was connected with the tragical story of the unfortunate André, who had been taken prisoner hard by[4]; and was universally known by the name of Major André's tree. The common people regarded it with a mixture of respect and superstition, partly out of[5] sympathy for the fate[6] of its ill-starred namesake[7], and partly from the tales of strange sights, and doleful[8] lamentations, told concerning it[9].

As Ichabod approached this fearful tree, he began to whistle; he thought his whistle was answered; it was but a blast sweeping sharply through[10] the dry branches. As he approached a little nearer, he thought he saw something white, hanging in the midst of the tree: he paused and ceased whistling but, on looking more narrowly[11], perceived that it was a place where the tree had been scathed by lightning[12], and the white wood laid bare[13]. Suddenly he heard a groan[14]—his teeth chattered, and his knees smote[15] against the saddle: it was but the rubbing of one huge bough[16] upon another, as they were swayed about[17] by the breeze. He passed the tree in safety, but new perils lay before him.

About two hundred yards from the tree, a small brook crossed the road, and ran into a marshy and thickly-wooded glen[18], known by the name of Wiley's Swamp. A few rough logs[19], laid side by side, served for a[20] bridge over this stream. On that side of the road where the brook entered

1. point de repère
2. branches
3. noueuses
4. tout près de là
5. par
6. sort
7. l'infortuné personnage qui lui avait donné son nom
8. de tristes
9. qu'on racontait à son sujet
10. ce n'était qu'une rafale traversant brusquement
11. attentivement
12. frappé par la foudre
13. était à nu
14. gémissement
15. cognèrent
16. frottement d'une grosse branche
17. chahutées
18. vallon
19. grossiers rondins
20. faisaient office de

1. entremêlés de
2. l'épreuve la plus rude
3. que s'étaient tenus cachés les vigoureux cavaliers
4. à la nuit tombée
5. battre
6. rassembla
7. une dizaine
8. s'élancer
9. vint heurter la rampe
10. ce contre-temps
11. tira les rênes
12. vigoureuse-ment
13. partit
14. ronces
15. d'aulnes
16. asséna alors des coups de
17. flancs décharnés
18. soufflant et renâclant
19. s'arrêta
20. bruit de pas s'enfonçant dans la boue
21. difforme
22. imposant
23. ne bougeait pas
24. recroquevillé

the wood, a group of oaks and chestnuts, matted thick with[1] wild grape-vines, threw a cavernous gloom over it. To pass this bridge was the severest trial[2]. It was at this identical spot that the unfortunate André was captured, and under the covert of those chestnuts and vines were the sturdy yeomen concealed[3] who surprised him. This has ever since been considered a haunted stream, and fearful are the feelings of the schoolboy who has to pass it alone after dark[4].

As he approached the stream, his heart began to thump[5]; he summoned up[6], however, all his resolution, gave his horse half a score[7] of kicks in the ribs, and attempted to dash briskly[8] across the bridge; but instead of starting forward, the perverse old animal made a lateral movement, and ran broadside against the fence[9]. Ichabod, whose fears increased with the delay[10], jerked the reins[11] on the other side, and kicked lustily[12] with the contrary foot: it was all in vain; his steed started[13], it is true, but it was only to plunge to the opposite side of the road into a thicket of brambles[14] and alder bushes[15]. The schoolmaster now bestowed both[16] whip and heel upon the starveling ribs[17] of old Gunpowder, who dashed forward, snuffling and snorting[18], but came to a stand[19] just by the bridge, with a suddenness that had nearly sent his rider sprawling over his head. Just at this moment a plashy tramp[20] by the side of the bridge caught the sensitive ear of Ichabod. In the dark shadow of the grove, on the margin of the brook, he beheld something huge, misshapen[21] and towering[22]. It stirred not[23], but seemed gathered up[24] in the gloom, like some gigantic monster ready to spring upon the traveller.

The hair of the affrighted pedagogue rose upon his head with terror. What was to be done? To turn and fly was now too late; and besides, what chance was there of escaping ghost or goblin, if such it was, which could ride upon the wings of the wind? Summoning up, therefore, a show[1] of courage, he demanded in stammering accents[2], "Who are you?" He received no reply. He repeated his demand in a still more agitated voice. Still there was no answer. Once more he cudgelled the sides[3] of the inflexible Gunpowder, and, shutting his eyes, broke forth[4] with involuntary fervor into a psalm tune[5]. Just then the shadowy object of alarm put itself in motion, and with a scramble and a bound[6] stood at once in the middle of the road. Though the night was dark and dismal, yet the form of the unknown might now in some degree be ascertained[7]. He appeared to be a horseman of large dimensions, and mounted on a black horse of powerful frame[8]. He made no offer of molestation[9] or sociability, but kept aloof[10] on one side of the road, jogging along on the blind side of old Gunpowder, who had now got over[11] his fright and waywardness[12].

Ichabod, who had no relish for[13] this strange midnight companion, and bethought himself of[14] the adventure of Brom Bones with the Galloping Hessian, now quickened his steed in hopes of leaving him behind. The stranger[15], however, quickened his horse to an equal pace[16]. Ichabod pulled up[17], and fell into a walk[18], thinking to lag[19] behind,—the other did the same. His heart began to sink within him[20]; he endeavored to resume[21] his psalm tune, but his parched[22] tongue clove to the roof of his mouth[23], and he could

1. semblant
2. en bégayant
3. fouetta les flancs
4. entonna
5. un psaume
6. d'un bond
7. discernée
8. carrure
9. ne manifesta aucune agressivité
10. à l'écart
11. s'était à présent remis de
12. de son obstination
13. n'appréciait guère
14. repensait à
15. inconnu
16. allure
17. ralentit
18. se mit au pas
19. rester
20. L'abattement l'envahit
21. s'efforça de reprendre
22. desséchée
23. lui collait au palais

not utter a stave[1]. There was something in the moody and dogged[2] silence of this pertinacious[3] companion that was mysterious and appalling[4]. It was soon fearfully accounted for[5]. On mounting a rising ground, which brought the figure of his fellow-traveller in relief against the sky, gigantic in height, and muffled[6] in a cloak[7], Ichabod was horror-struck on perceiving that he was headless!—but his horror was still more increased on observing that the head, which should have rested on his shoulders, was carried before him on the pommel of his saddle! His terror rose to desperation; he rained a shower[8] of kicks and blows upon Gunpowder, hoping by a sudden movement to give his companion the slip[9]; but the spectre started full jump[10] with him. Away, then, they dashed through thick and thin[11]; stones flying and sparks flashing at every bound[12]. Ichabod's flimsy garments[13] fluttered in the air, as he stretched his long lank body away over his horse's head, in the eagerness of his flight.

They had now reached the road which turns off to Sleepy Hollow; but Gunpowder, who seemed possessed with a demon, instead of keeping up it[14], made an opposite turn, and plunged headlong[15] downhill to the left. This road leads through a sandy hollow shaded by trees for about a quarter of a mile, where it crosses the bridge famous in goblin story; and just beyond swells the green knoll[16] on which stands the whitewashed church.

As yet[17] the panic of the steed had given his unskilful[18] rider an apparent advantage in the chase[19], but just as he had got half way through the hollow, the girths[20] of the saddle gave way[21],

1. émettre la moindre note
2. tenace
3. entêté
4. terrible
5. Il comprit bientôt pourquoi, hélas
6. emmitouflé
7. manteau
8. fit pleuvoir une volée
9. échapper à son compagnon
10. s'élança
11. à bride abattue
12. bond
13. Les maigres vêtements
14. la suivre
15. tête baissée
16. se dresse la colline verte
17. Jusque-là,
18. piètre
19. poursuite
20. sangles
21. cédèrent

and he felt it slipping from under him. He seized it by the pommel, and endeavored[1] to hold it firm, but in vain; and had just time to save himself by clasping[2] old Gunpowder round the neck, when the saddle fell to the earth, and he heard it trampled under foot by his pursuer. For a moment the terror of Hans Van Ripper's wrath[3] passed across his mind,—for it was his Sunday saddle; but this was no time for petty[4] fears; the goblin was hard on his haunches[5]; and (unskilful rider that he was!) he had much ado[6] to maintain his seat; sometimes slipping on one side, sometimes on another, and sometimes jolted[7] on the high ridge of his horse's backbone[8], with a violence that he verily feared would cleave him asunder[9].

An opening in the trees now cheered him with the hopes[10] that the church bridge was at hand[11]. The wavering reflection[12] of a silver star in the bosom of the brook told him that he was not mistaken. He saw the walls of the church dimly glaring under the trees beyond. He recollected[13] the place where Brom Bones's ghostly competitor had disappeared. "If I can but[14] reach that bridge," thought Ichabod, "I am safe." Just then he heard the black steed panting[15] and blowing close[16] behind him; he even fancied[17] that he felt his hot breath. Another convulsive kick in the ribs, and old Gunpowder sprang upon the bridge; he thundered[18] over the resounding planks; he gained the opposite side; and now Ichabod cast a look behind to see if his pursuer should vanish, according to rule, in a flash of fire and brimstone[19]. Just then he saw the goblin rising in his stirrups[20], and in the very act of hurling[21] his head at him. Ichabod endeavored to dodge[22] the horrible mis-

1. s'efforça
2. en serrant
3. le courroux
4. insignifiantes
5. juste derrière lui
6. à faire
7. secoué
8. garrot de sa monture
9. telle qu'il craignit vraiment d'être coupé en deux
10. lui fit espérer
11. proche
12. reflet vacillant
13. se souvint de
14. parviens à
15. haleter
16. juste
17. s'imagina même
18. ses sabots retentirent
19. de soufre
20. se dresser sur ses étriers
21. s'apprêter à lancer
22. esquiver

sile, but too late. It encountered his cranium with a tremendous crash,—he was tumbled headlong[1] into the dust, and Gunpowder, the black steed, and the goblin rider, passed by like a whirlwind[2].

The next morning the old horse was found without his saddle, and with the bridle[3] under his feet, soberly cropping[4] the grass at his master's gate. Ichabod did not make his appearance at breakfast; dinner-hour came, but no Ichabod. The boys assembled at the schoolhouse, and strolled idly about the banks[5] of the brook; but no schoolmaster. Hans Van Ripper now began to feel some uneasiness[6] about the fate of poor Ichabod, and his saddle. An inquiry[7] was set on foot, and after diligent investigation they came upon his traces. In one part of the road leading to the church was found the saddle trampled in the dirt[8]; the tracks of horses' hoofs deeply dented[9] in the road, and evidently at furious speed, were traced to the[10] bridge, beyond which, on the bank of a broad part of the brook, where the water ran deep and black, was found the hat of the unfortunate Ichabod, and close beside it a shattered[11] pumpkin[12].

The brook was searched, but the body of the schoolmaster was not to be discovered. Hans Van Ripper as executor of his estate[13], examined the bundle[14] which contained all his worldly effects[15]. They consisted of two shirts and a half; two stocks[16] for the neck; a pair or two of worsted stockings[17]; an old pair of corduroy smallclothes[18]; a rusty razor; a book of psalm tunes full of dog's-ears[19]; and a broken pitch-pipe[20]. As to the books and furniture of the schoolhouse, they belonged to the community, excepting Cotton Mather's *History of Witchcraft*, a *New England*

1. tomba la tête la première
2. tourbillon
3. bride
4. broutant tranquillement
5. flânèrent paresseusement le long des berges
6. inquiétude
7. enquête
8. piétinée, à terre
9. marquées
10. suivies jusqu'au
11. éclatée
12. citrouillle
13. en tant qu'exécuteur testamentaire
14. ballot
15. biens matériels
16. foulards
17. bas de laine
18. culottes en velours côtelé
19. pages écornées
20. diapason

Almanac, and a book of dreams and fortune-telling[1]; in which last was a sheet of foolscap[2] much scribbled and blotted[3] in several fruitless attempts to make a copy of verses in honor of the heiress of Van Tassel. These magic books and the poetic scrawl[4] were forthwith[5] consigned to the flames[6] by Hans Van Ripper; who, from that time forward, determined to send his children no more to school, observing that he never knew any good come of this same[7] reading and writing. Whatever money the schoolmaster possessed, and he had received his quarter's pay[8] but[9] a day or two before, he must have had about his person[10] at the time of his disappearance.

The mysterious event caused much speculation at the church on the following Sunday. Knots of gazers and gossips[11] were collected[12] in the churchyard, at the bridge, and at the spot where the hat and pumpkin had been found. The stories of Brouwer, of Bones, and a whole budget of others[13] were called to mind[14]; and when they had diligently considered them all, and compared them with the symptoms of the present case, they shook their heads, and came to the conclusion that Ichabod had been carried off by the Galloping Hessian. As he was a bachelor[15], and in nobody's debt[16], nobody troubled his head any more about[17] him; the school was removed to a different quarter of the hollow, and another pedagogue reigned in his stead[18].

It is true, an old farmer, who had been down to New York on a visit several years after, and from whom this account of the ghostly adventure was received, brought home the intelligence that[19] Ichabod Crane was still alive; that he had left the

1. divination
2. papier ministre
3. taché
4. lignes griffonnées
5. sur-le-champ
6. jetés au feu
7. genre de
8. paie du trimestre
9. à peine
10. devait l'avoir sur lui
11. Des groupes de badauds et de commères
12. se formèrent
13. bien d'autres
14. rappelées
15. célibataire
16. ne devait rien à personne
17. ne se préoccupa plus de
18. place
19. rapporta que

neighborhood partly through fear of the goblin and Hans Van Ripper, and partly in mortification at having been suddenly dismissed[1] by the heiress; that he had changed[2] his quarters to a distant part of the country; had kept school and studied law at the same time; had been admitted to the bar[3]; turned politician; electioneered[4]; written for the newspapers; and finally had been made a justice[5] of the Ten Pound Court. Brom Bones, too, who, shortly after his rival's disappearance conducted the blooming Katrina in triumph to the altar[6], was observed to look exceedingly knowing[7] whenever the story of Ichabod was related, and always burst into a hearty laugh at the mention of the pumpkin; which led some to suspect that he knew more about the matter than he chose to tell.

The old country wives, however, who are the best judges of these matters, maintain to this day that Ichabod was spirited away[8] by supernatural means; and it is a favorite story often told about the neighborhood round the winter evening fire. The bridge became more than ever an object of superstitious awe[9]; and that may be the reason why the road has been altered of late years[10], so as to approach the church by the border of the millpond. The schoolhouse being deserted soon fell to decay[11], and was reported to be haunted by the ghost of the unfortunate pedagogue and the plowboy[12], loitering homeward[13] of a still summer evening[14], has often fancied his voice at a distance, chanting a melancholy psalm tune among the tranquil solitudes of Sleepy Hollow.

1. si brutalement éconduit
2. établi
3. barreau
4. avait mené une campagne électorale
5. nommé juge
6. à l'autel
7. avait un air étrangement entendu
8. enlevé
9. crainte
10. modifiée il y a quelques années
11. en ruine
12. laboureur
13. rentrant tranquillement chez lui
14. les soirs d'été

POSTSCRIPT

Found in the Handwriting of Mr. Knickerbocker.

The preceding tale is given almost in the precise words in which I heard it related at a Corporation meeting at the ancient city of Manhattoes, at which were present many of its sagest and most illustrious burghers[1]. The narrator was a pleasant, shabby[2], gentlemanly old fellow, in pepper-and-salt clothes, with a sadly humourous face, and one whom I strongly suspected of being poor—he made such efforts to be entertaining[3]. When his story was concluded, there was much laughter and approbation, particularly from two or three deputy aldermen[4], who had been asleep the greater part of the time. There was, however, one tall, dry-looking old gentleman, with beetling eyebrows[5], who maintained a grave and rather severe face throughout[6], now and then folding his arms, inclining his head, and looking down upon the floor, as if turning a doubt over[7] in his mind. He was one of your wary men[8], who never laugh but upon good grounds[9]—when they have reason and law on their side. When the mirth[10] of the rest of the company had subsided[11], and silence was restored, he leaned one arm on the elbow of his chair, and sticking the other akimbo[12], demanded, with a slight, but exceedingly sage

1. citoyens

2. un peu miteux

3. divertissant

4. conseillers municipaux

5. aux sourcils proéminents

6. tout du long

7. comme s'il ruminait un doute

8. ces hommes prudents

9. ne rient jamais sans une bonne raison

10. l'hilarité

11. se fut calmée

12. mettant l'autre poing sur la hanche

motion of the head, and contraction of the brow[1], what was the moral of the story, and what it went to prove?

The story-teller, who was just putting a glass of wine to his lips, as a refreshment after his toils[2], paused for a moment, looked at his inquirer with an air of infinite deference, and, lowering the glass slowly to the table, observed that the story was intended most logically to prove—

"That there is no situation in life but has[3] its advantages and pleasures—provided we will but take a joke as we find it[4]:

"That, therefore, he that[5] runs races with goblin troopers[6] is likely to have rough riding of it[7].

"Ergo[8], for a country schoolmaster to be refused the hand of a Dutch heiress is a certain step to high preferment[9] in the state."

The cautious old gentleman knit his brows tenfold closer[10] after this explanation, being sorely puzzled[11] by the ratiocination of the syllogism[12], while, methought[13], the one in pepper-and-salt eyed him with something of a triumphant leer[14]. At length[15] he observed that all this was very well, but still he thought the story a little on the[16] extravagant—there were one or two points on which he had his doubts.

"Faith[17], sir," replied the story-teller, "as to that matter, I don't believe one-half of it myself."

D. K.

1. plissement du front
2. efforts
3. qui n'ait
4. à condition qu'on prenne la plaisanterie comme elle vient
5. celui qui
6. des fantômes
7. susceptible de passer un mauvais quart d'heure
8. Par conséquent
9. promotion sociale
10. fronça davantage les sourcils
11. très peu convaincu
12. subtilité du syllogisme
13. me semble-t-il
14. [mauvais] regard
15. Finalement
16. quelque peu
17. Ma foi

THE BROWN HAND

by Arthur Conan Doyle

EVERYONE knows that Sir Dominick Holden, the famous Indian[1] surgeon[2], made me his heir[3], and that his death changed me in an hour from a hard-working and impecunious young man to a well-to-do[4] landed[5] proprietor. Many know also that there were at least five people between the inheritance[6] and me, and that Sir Dominick's selection appeared to be altogether[7] arbitrary and whimsical[8]. I can assure them, however, that they are quite mistaken, and that, although I only knew Sir Dominick in the closing[9] years of his life, there were, none the less, very real reasons why he should show his goodwill[10] towards me. As a matter of fact, though I say it myself, no man ever did more for another than I did for my Indian uncle. I cannot expect the story to be believed, but it is so singular that I should feel that it was a breach of duty[11] if I did not put it upon record[12]—so here it is, and your belief or incredulity is your own affair.

Sir Dominick Holden, CB[13], KCSI[14], and I don't know what besides, was the most distinguished[15] Indian surgeon of his day. In the Army originally, he afterwards settled down into civil practice in Bombay, and visited, as a consultant, every

1. des Indes
2. chirurgien
3. a fait de moi son héritier
4. riche
5. terrien
6. héritage
7. à la fois
8. capricieuse
9. dernières
10. bienveillance
11. croirais manquer à mes devoirs
12. n'en faisais pas le récit
13. [Companion of the Order of the Bath]
14. [Knight Commander of the Order of the Star of India]
15. éminent

part of India. His name is best remembered in connection with the Oriental Hospital, which he founded and supported. The time came, however, when his iron constitution began to show signs of the long strain[1] to which he had subjected it, and his brother practitioners[2] (who were not, perhaps, entirely disinterested upon the point) were unanimous in recommending him to return to England. He held on so long as he could, but at last he developed nervous symptoms of a very pronounced character, and so came back, a broken man, to his native county of Wiltshire. He bought a considerable estate[3] with an ancient manor-house upon the edge of Salisbury Plain, and devoted his old age to the study of Comparative Pathology, which had been his learned[4] hobby all his life, and in which he was a foremost authority[5].

We of the family were, as may be imagined, much excited by the news of the return of this rich and childless uncle to England. On his part, although by no means exuberant in his hospitality, he showed some sense of his duty to his relations[6], and each of us in turn had an invitation to visit him. From the accounts[7] of my cousins it appeared to be a melancholy business[8], and it was with mixed feelings that I at last received my own summons to appear[9] at Rodenhurst. My wife was so carefully excluded in the invitation that my first impulse was to refuse it, but the interests of the children had to be considered, and so, with her consent, I set out one October afternoon upon my visit to Wiltshire, with little thought[10] of what that visit was to entail[11].

My uncle's estate was situated where the arable land of the plains begins to swell upwards

1. tension
2. confrères
3. domaine
4. savant
5. expert de premier ordre
6. envers sa famille
7. D'après les récits
8. occasion
9. invitation
10. sans me douter
11. allait supposer

into the rounded chalk hills[1] which are characteristic of the county. As I drove from Dinton Station in the waning[2] light of that autumn day, I was impressed by the weird[3] nature of the scenery. The few scattered cottages of the peasants were so dwarfed[4] by the huge evidences[5] of prehistoric life, that the present appeared to be a dream and the past to be the obtrusive and masterful reality. The road wound[6] through the valleys, formed by a succession of grassy hills, and the summit of each was cut and carved[7] into the most elaborate[8] fortifications, some circular, and some square, but all on a scale which has defied the winds and the rains of many centuries. Some call them Roman and some British, but their true origin and the reasons for this particular tract[9] of country being so interlaced with entrenchments have never been finally made clear. Here and there on the long, smooth, olive-coloured slopes[10] there rose small, rounded barrows or tumuli[11]. Beneath them lie the cremated ashes of the race which cut so deeply into the hills, but their graves tell us nothing save[12] that a jar full of dust represents the man who once laboured under the sun.

It was through this weird country that I approached my uncle's residence of Rodenhurst, and the house was, as I found, in due keeping[13] with its surroundings. Two broken and weather-stained pillars, each surmounted by a mutilated heraldic emblem, flanked the entrance to a neglected drive[14]. A cold wind whistled through the elms[15] which lined it, and the air was full of the drifting leaves. At the far end, under the gloomy arch of trees, a single yellow lamp burned steadily. In the dim half-light of the coming night I saw

1. s'élève en collines de craie
2. déclinante
3. étrange
4. écrasés
5. vestiges
6. serpentait
7. sculptée
8. en complexes
9. portion
10. versants
11. des tumulus
12. hormis
13. en accord
14. allée
15. ormes

a long, low building stretching out two irregular wings, with deep eaves[1], a sloping gambrel roof[2], and walls which were criss-crossed with[3] timber balks[4] in the fashion of the Tudors. The cheery light of a fire flickered in the broad, latticed[5] window to the left of the low-porched door, and this, as it proved, marked the study of my uncle, for it was thither[6] that I was led by his butler in order to make my host's acquaintance.

He was cowering[7] over his fire, for the moist chill[8] of an English autumn had set him shivering. His lamp was unlit, and I only saw the red glow of the embers[9] beating upon a huge, craggy[10] face, with a Red Indian nose and cheek, and deep furrows[11] and seams[12] from eye to chin, the sinister marks of hidden volcanic fires. He sprang up at my entrance with something of an old-world[13] courtesy and welcomed me warmly to Rodenhurst. At the same time I was conscious, as the lamp was carried in, that it was a very critical pair of light-blue eyes which looked out at me from under shaggy eyebrows[14], like scouts[15] beneath a bush, and that this outlandish[16] uncle of mine was carefully reading off my character with all the ease of a practised observer and an experienced man of the world.

For my part I looked at him, and looked again, for I had never seen a man whose appearance was more fitted[17] to hold one's attention. His figure was the framework[18] of a giant, but he had fallen away until[19] his coat dangled straight down in a shocking fashion from a pair of broad and bony shoulders[20]. All his limbs[21] were huge yet emaciated, and I could not take my gaze from his knobby[22] wrists, and long, gnarled[23] hands. But

1. avant-toits
2. toit à double pente douce
3. zébrés de
4. poutres
5. à croisillons
6. là
7. se blotissait
8. froideur humide
9. braises
10. anguleux
11. sillons
12. coutures
13. surannée
14. sourcils broussailleux
15. des éclaireurs
16. exotique
17. fût plus digne
18. Il avait la carrure
19. tellement maigri que
20. pendait terriblement de ses larges épaules osseuses
21. Bras et jambes
22. noueux
23. tordues

his eyes—those peering[1], light-blue eyes—they were the most arrestive[2] of any of his peculiarities. It was not their colour alone, nor was it the ambush of hair[3] in which they lurked[4]; but it was the expression which I read in them. For the appearance and bearing[5] of the man were masterful, and one expected a certain corresponding arrogance in his eyes, but instead of that I read the look which tells of a spirit cowed and crushed[6], the furtive, expectant look of the dog whose master has taken the whip[7] from the rack[8]. I formed my own medical diagnosis upon one glance at those critical and yet appealing eyes. I believed that he was stricken with some mortal ailment, that he knew himself to be exposed to sudden death, and that he lived in terror of it. Such was my judgment—a false one, as the event showed[9]; but I mention it that it may help you to realize the look which I read in his eyes.

My uncle's welcome was, as I have said, a courteous one, and in an hour or so I found myself seated between him and his wife at a comfortable dinner, with curious, pungent delicacies[10] upon the table, and a stealthy[11], quick-eyed Oriental waiter behind his chair. The old couple had come round to that tragic imitation of the dawn of life when husband and wife, having lost or scattered[12] all those who were their intimates, find themselves face to face and alone once more, their work done, and the end nearing fast. Those who have reached that stage[13] in sweetness and love, who can change their winter into a gentle, Indian summer, have come as victors through the ordeal of life[14]. Lady Holden was a small, alert woman with a kindly eye[15], and her expression

1. perçants
2. frappantes
3. masse de cheveux
4. semblaient se tapir
5. le maintien
6. anéanti
7. fouet
8. de son râtelier
9. comme la suite le montra
10. plats fins fortement épicés
11. furtif
12. éparpillé
13. étape
14. ont triomphé des épreuves de la vie
15. au regard doux

as she glanced at him was a certificate of character[1] to her husband. And yet, though I read a mutual love in their glances, I read also mutual horror, and recognized in her face some reflection[2] of that stealthy fear which I had detected in his. Their talk was sometimes merry and sometimes sad, but there was a forced note in their merriment and a naturalness in their sadness which told me that a heavy heart beat upon either side of me[3].

We were sitting over our first glass of wine, and the servants had left the room, when the conversation took a turn which produced a remarkable effect upon my host and hostess. I cannot recall[4] what it was which started the topic of the supernatural, but it ended in my showing them that the abnormal in psychical experiences was a subject to which I had, like many neurologists, devoted[5] a great deal of attention. I concluded by narrating my experiences when, as a member of the Psychical Research Society, I had formed one[6] of a committee of three who spent the night in a haunted house. Our adventures were neither exciting nor convincing, but, such as it was, the story appeared to interest my auditors in a remarkable degree. They listened with an eager[7] silence, and I caught a look of intelligence between them[8] which I could not understand. Lady Holden immediately afterwards rose and left the room.

Sir Dominick pushed the cigar-box over to me, and we smoked for some little time in silence. That huge, bony hand of his was twitching[9] as he raised it with his cheroot[10] to his lips, and I felt that the man's nerves were vibrating like fiddle-strings[11]. My instincts told me that he was

1. moralité
2. un reflet
3. chez mes deux commensaux
4. ne me souviens pas de
5. consacré
6. avais fait partie
7. très attentif
8. les vis s'échanger un regard de complicité
9. tremblait légèrement
10. cigare
11. à vif

on the verge[1] of some intimate confidence, and I feared to speak lest I should interrupt it. At last he turned towards me with a spasmodic gesture like a man who throws his last scruple to the winds[2].

"From the little that I have seen of you it appears to me, Dr. Hardacre," said he, "that you are the very man[3] I have wanted to meet."

"I am delighted to hear it, sir."

"Your head seems to be cool and steady[4]. You will acquit me of any desire to flatter you, for the circumstances are too serious to permit of insincerities. You have some special knowledge[5] upon these subjects, and you evidently view them from that philosophical standpoint which robs them of all vulgar terror. I presume that the sight of an apparition would not seriously discompose you?"

"I think not, sir."

"Would even interest you, perhaps?"

"Most intensely."

"As a psychical observer, you would probably investigate it in as impersonal a fashion as an astronomer investigates a wandering comet[6]?"

"Precisely."

He gave a heavy sigh.

"Believe me, Dr. Hardacre, there was a time when I could have spoken as you do now. My nerve was a byword[7] in India. Even the Mutiny[8] never shook it for an instant. And yet you see what I am reduced to—the most timorous man, perhaps, in all this county of Wiltshire. Do not speak too bravely upon this subject, or you may find yourself subjected to as long-drawn a test[9] as I am—a test which can only end in the madhouse[10] or the grave[11]."

1. sur le point
2. aux quatre vents
3. précisément l'homme que
4. Vous semblez ferme et plein de sang-froid
5. connaissance
6. étoile filante
7. réputé
8. révolte des cipayes [1857]
9. mis à l'épreuve aussi longtemps
10. à l'asile
11. dans la tombe

I waited patiently until he should see fit[1] to go farther in his confidence[2]. His preamble had, I need not say, filled me with interest and expectation.

"For some years, Dr. Hardacre," he continued, "my life and that of my wife have been made miserable[3] by a cause which is so grotesque that it borders upon the ludicrous[4]. And yet familiarity has never made it more easy to bear—on the contrary, as time passes[5] my nerves become more worn and shattered[6] by the constant attrition[7]. If you have no physical fears, Dr. Hardacre, I should very much value your opinion upon this phenomenon which troubles us so."

"For what it is worth[8] my opinion is entirely at your service. May I ask the nature of the phenomenon?"

"I think that your experiences will have a higher evidential[9] value if you are not told in advance what you may expect to encounter. You are yourself aware of[10] the quibbles[11] of unconscious cerebration and subjective impressions with which a scientific sceptic may throw a doubt upon your statement[12]. It would be as well to guard against them in advance[13]."

"What shall I do, then?"

"I will tell you. Would you mind following me this way?" He led me out of the dining-room and down a long passage until we came to a terminal door. Inside there was a large, bare[14] room fitted as a[15] laboratory, with numerous scientific instruments and bottles. A shelf[16] ran along one side, upon which there stood a long line of glass jars[17] containing pathological and anatomical specimens.

1. jugeât bon
2. de continuer ses confidences
3. assombries
4. frise le ridicule
5. avec le temps,
6. sont plus fortement ébranlés
7. usure
8. Pour ce qu'elle vaut,
9. de preuve
10. connaissez
11. chicanes
12. jeter le discrédit sur vos affirmations
13. de s'en prémunir
14. vide
15. aménagée en
16. étagère
17. bocaux en verre

"You see that I still dabble[1] in some of my old studies," said Sir Dominick. "These jars are the remains of what was once a most excellent collection, but unfortunately I lost the greater part of them when my house was burned down in Bombay in '92. It was a most unfortunate affair for me—in more ways than one. I had examples of many rare conditions[2], and my splenic[3] collection was probably unique. These are the survivors."

I glanced over them, and saw that they really were of a very great value and rarity from a pathological point of view: bloated[4] organs, gaping cysts[5], distorted bones, odious parasites—a singular exhibition of the products of India.

"There is, as you see, a small settee[6] here," said my host. "It was far from our intention to offer a guest so meagre an accommodation[7], but since affairs have taken this turn, it would be a great kindness upon your part if you would consent to spend the night in this apartment[8]. I beg that you will not hesitate to let me know if the idea should be at all repugnant to you."

"On the contrary," I said, "it is most acceptable."

"My own room is the second on the left, so that if you should feel that you are in need of company a call would always bring me to your side."

"I trust[9] that I shall not be compelled to disturb you[10]."

"It is unlikely that I shall be asleep. I do not sleep much. Do not hesitate to summon me."

And so with this agreement we joined Lady Holden in the drawing-room and talked of lighter[11] things.

1. plonge encore à l'occasion
2. maladies
3. de rates [organe]
4. boursouflés
5. des vessies béantes
6. canapé
7. un logement si fruste
8. pièce
9. espère bien
10. ne pas avoir à vous déranger
11. moins graves

It was no affectation upon my part to say that the prospect[1] of my night's adventure was an agreeable one. I have no pretence to[2] greater physical courage than my neighbours, but familiarity with a subject robs it of those vague and undefined terrors which are the most appalling[3] to the imaginative mind. The human brain[4] is capable of only one strong emotion at a time, and if it be filled with[5] curiosity or scientific enthusiasm, there is no room for fear. It is true that I had my uncle's assurance that he had himself originally taken this point of view, but I reflected that the break-down of his nervous system might be due to his forty years in India as much as to any psychical experiences which had befallen him[6]. I at least was sound[7] in nerve and brain, and it was with something of the pleasurable thrill of anticipation with which the sportsman takes his position beside the haunt of his game[8] that I shut the laboratory door behind me, and partially undressing, lay down upon the rug-covered settee.

It was not an ideal atmosphere for a bedroom. The air was heavy with many chemical odours, that of methylated spirit predominating. Nor were the decorations of my chamber very sedative. The odious line of glass jars with their relics of disease and suffering stretched[9] in front of my very eyes[10]. There was no blind[11] to the window, and a three-quarter moon streamed its white light into the room, tracing a silver square with filigree lattices[12] upon the opposite wall. When I had extinguished my candle this one bright patch[13] in the midst of the general gloom had certainly an eerie[14] and discomposing aspect. A rigid and absolute silence reigned throughout the old house,

1. perspective
2. ne prétends pas avoir
3. effrayants
4. cerveau
5. s'il est plein de
6. qui lui fussent arrivées
7. sain
8. le chasseur guette sa proie
9. s'étendait
10. sous mes yeux
11. aucun store
12. des croisillons en filigrane
13. unique tache lumineuse
14. inquiétant

so that the low swish[1] of the branches in the garden came softly and smoothly to my ears. It may have been the hypnotic lullaby[2] of this gentle susurrus[3], or it may have been the result of my tiring day, but after many dozings[4] and many efforts to regain my clearness of perception, I fell at last into a deep and dreamless sleep.

I was awakened[5] by some sound in the room, and I instantly raised myself upon my elbow on the couch. Some hours had passed, for the square patch upon the wall had slid downwards and sideways[6] until it lay obliquely at the end of my bed. The rest of the room was in deep shadow. At first I could see nothing, presently[7], as my eyes became accustomed to the faint light, I was aware[8], with a thrill which all my scientific absorption could not entirely prevent, that something was moving slowly[9] along the line of the wall. A gentle, shuffling sound[10], as of soft slippers, came to my ears, and I dimly[11] discerned a human figure[12] walking stealthily[13] from the direction of the door. As it emerged into the patch of moonlight I saw very clearly what it was and how it was employed. It was a man, short and squat[14], dressed in some sort of dark-grey gown[15], which hung straight from his shoulders to his feet. The moon shone upon the side of his face, and I saw that it was chocolate-brown in colour[16], with a ball of black hair like a woman's at the back of his head. He walked slowly, and his eyes were cast upwards towards the line of bottles which contained those gruesome[17] remnants of humanity. He seemed to examine each jar with attention, and then to pass on to the next. When he had come to the end of the line, immediately op-

1. bruissement
2. bercement
3. doux chuchotis
4. assoupissements
5. réveillé
6. s'était écarté vers le bas
7. puis
8. perçus
9. un mouvement lent
10. glissement
11. vaguement
12. silhouette
13. à pas de velours
14. petit et trapu
15. robe
16. de couleur marron
17. macabres

posite my bed, he stopped, faced me, threw up his hands with a gesture of despair, and vanished from my sight.

I have said that he threw up his hands, but I should have said his arms, for[1] as he assumed[2] that attitude of despair I observed a singular peculiarity[3] about his appearance. He had only one hand! As the sleeves drooped down from the upflung arms[4] I saw the left plainly, but the right ended in a knobby and unsightly stump[5]. In every other way his appearance was so natural, and I had both seen and heard him so clearly, that I could easily have believed that he was an Indian servant of Sir Dominick's who had come into my room in search of something. It was only his sudden disappearance which suggested anything more sinister to me. As it was[6] I sprang from my couch, lit a candle, and examined the whole room carefully. There were no signs of my visitor, and I was forced to conclude that there had really been something outside the normal laws of Nature in his appearance[7]. I lay awake for the remainder of the night, but nothing else occurred to disturb me.

I am an early riser, but my uncle was an even earlier one, for I found him pacing up and down the lawn[8] at the side of the house. He ran towards me in his eagerness[9] when he saw me come out from the door.

"Well, well!" he cried. "Did you see him?"

"An Indian with one hand?"

"Precisely."

"Yes, I saw him"—and I told him all that occurred. When I had finished, he led the way into his study.

1. car,
2. lorsqu'il prit
3. détail étrange
4. sur ses bras levés en l'air,
5. en un moignon disgracieux
6. Quoi qu'il en soit,
7. d'apparence contraire aux lois de la nature
8. arpentant la pelouse
9. impatience

"We have a little time before breakfast," said he. "It will suffice to give you an explanation of this extraordinary affair—so far as I can explain that which is essentially inexplicable. In the first place, when I tell you that for four years I have never passed one single night, either in Bombay, aboard ship[1], or here in England without my sleep being broken by this fellow, you will understand why it is that I am a wreck of my former self[2]. His programme is always the same. He appears by my bedside, shakes me roughly by the shoulder, passes from my room into the laboratory, walks slowly along the line of my bottles, and then vanishes. For more than a thousand times he has gone through the same routine."

"What does he want?"

"He wants his hand."

"His hand?"

"Yes, it came about in this way. I was summoned[3] to Peshawur for a consultation some ten years ago, and while there I was asked to look at the hand of a native who was passing through with an Afghan caravan. The fellow came from some mountain tribe living away at the back of beyond[4] somewhere on the other side of Kaffiristan. He talked a bastard Pushtoo[5], and it was all I could do to understand him. He was suffering from a soft sarcomatous swelling of[6] one of the metacarpal joints[7], and I made him realize that it was only by losing his hand that he could hope to save his life. After much persuasion he consented to the operation, and he asked me, when it was over, what fee[8] I demanded. The poor fellow was almost a beggar[9], so that the idea of a fee was absurd, but I answered in jest[10] that

1. à bord d'un bateau

2. je ne suis plus que l'ombre de moi-même

3. appelé

4. au milieu de nulle part,

5. pachtoune [afghan]

6. œdème sarcomateux [cancéreux] sur

7. articulations

8. quels honoraires

9. mendiant

10. pour plaisanter

my fee should be his hand, and that I proposed to add it to my pathological collection.

"To my surprise he **demurred very much to**[1] the suggestion, and he explained that according to his religion it was an all-important matter that the body should be reunited after death, and so make a perfect **dwelling**[2] for the spirit. The belief is, of course, an old one, and the **mummies**[3] of the Egyptians arose from an analogous superstition. I answered him that his hand was already **off**[4], and asked him how he intended to preserve it. He replied that he **would pickle it in salt**[5] and **carry it about with him**[6]. I suggested that it might be safer **in my keeping than in his**[7], and that I had better **means**[8] than salt for **preserving it**[9]. On realizing that I really intended to carefully keep it, his opposition vanished instantly. 'But remember, sahib,' said he, 'I shall want it back when I **am dead**[10].' I laughed at the remark, and so the matter ended. I returned to my practice, and he no doubt in the course of time was able to continue his **journey**[11] to Afghanistan.

"Well, as I told you last night, I had a bad fire in my house at Bombay. Half of it was burned down, and, amongst other things, my pathological collection was largely destroyed. What you see are the poor remains of it. The hand of the hillman went with the rest, but I gave the matter no particular thought at the time. That was six years ago.

"Four years ago—two years after the fire—I was awakened one night by a furious **tugging**[12] at my sleeve. I sat up under the impression that my favourite mastiff was trying to arouse me. Instead of this, I saw my Indian patient of long

1. s'opposa à
2. résidence
3. momies
4. coupée
5. la couvrirait de sel
6. la garderait sur lui
7. que je la garde, moi
8. moyens
9. la conserver
10. serai mort
11. voyage
12. tiraillement

ago, dressed in the long, grey gown which was the badge[1] of his people. He was holding up his stump[2] and looking reproachfully at me. He then went over to my bottles, which at that time I kept in my room, and he examined them carefully, after which he gave a gesture of anger and vanished. I realized that he had just died[3], and that he had come to claim[4] my promise that I should keep his limb[5] in safety for him.

"Well, there you have it all, Dr Hardacre. Every night at the same hour for four years this performance[6] has been repeated. It is a simple thing in itself, but it has worn me out[7] like water dropping on a stone[8]. It has brought a vile insomnia with it, for I cannot sleep now for the expectation of his coming[9]. It has poisoned my old age and that of my wife, who has been the sharer in[10] this great trouble. But there is the breakfast gong, and she will be waiting impatiently to know how it fared with you last night[11]. We are both much indebted to you for your gallantry[12], for it takes something from the weight[13] of our misfortune when we share it, even for a single night, with a friend, and it reassures us to our sanity[14], which we are sometimes driven to question[15]."

This was the curious narrative which Sir Dominick confided to me—a story which to many would have appeared to be a grotesque impossibility, but which, after my experience of the night before, and my previous knowledge of such things, I was prepared to accept as an absolute fact. I thought deeply over the matter, and brought the whole range of my reading and experience to bear over it. After breakfast, I sur-

1. la marque
2. moignon
3. venait de mourir
4. réclamer l'exécution de
5. de garder sa main
6. spectacle
7. m'a épuisé,
8. un ruissellement sur la pierre
9. puisque j'attends sa venue
10. subi également
11. vous avez passé la nuit
12. vaillance généreuse
13. poids
14. quant à notre raison
15. dont nous doutons parfois

prised my host and hostess by announcing that I was returning to London by the next train.

"My dear doctor," cried Sir Dominick in great distress, "you make me feel that I have been guilty of a gross breach of hospitality in intruding this unfortunate matter upon you. I should have borne my own burden."

"It is, indeed, that matter which is taking me to London," I answered; "but you are mistaken, I assure you, if you think that my experience of last night was an unpleasant one to me. On the contrary, I am about to ask your permission to return in the evening and spend one more night in your laboratory. I am very eager[1] to see this visitor once again."

1. désireux

My uncle was exceedingly anxious to know what I was about to do, but my fears of raising false hopes prevented me from telling him. I was back in my own consulting-room a little after luncheon, and was confirming my memory of a passage in a recent book upon occultism which had arrested my attention when I read it.

"In the case of earth-bound[2] spirits," said my authority, "some one[3] dominant idea obsessing them at the hour of death is sufficient to hold them[4] in this material world. They are the amphibia of this life and of the next, capable of passing from one to the other as the turtle passes from land to water. The causes which may bind[5] a soul[6] so strongly to a life which its body has abandoned are any violent emotion. Avarice, revenge, anxiety, love, and pity have all been known to have this effect. As a rule it springs from some unfulfilled

2. terrestres
3. une seule
4. pour les retenir
5. enchaîner
6. âme

wish, and when the wish has been fulfilled the material bond relaxes. There are many cases upon record[1] which show the singular persistence of these visitors, and also their disappearance when their wishes have been fulfilled, or in some cases when a reasonable compromise has been effected."

1. On recense de nombreux cas

"*A reasonable compromise effected*"— those were the words which I had brooded over[2] all the morning, and which I now verified in the original. No actual atonement[3] could be made here—but a reasonable compromise! I made my way as fast as a train could take me to the Shadwell Seamen's Hospital, where my old friend Jack Hewett was house-surgeon[4]. Without explaining the situation I made him understand what it was that I wanted.

2. que j'avais ressassés

3. réparation réelle

4. chirurgien résident

"A brown[5] man's hand!" said he, in amazement. "What in the world do you want that for?"

5. à la peau mate

"Never mind. I'll tell you some day. I know that your wards[6] are full of Indians."

6. salles de soins

"I should think so. But a hand——" He thought a little, and then struck a bell.

"Travers," said he to a student-dresser[7], "what became of the hands of the lascar[8] which we took off yesterday? I mean the fellow from the East India Dock who got caught[9] in the steam winch[10]."

7. assistant chirurgien

8. l'Indien

9. s'est coincé

10. treuil à vapeur

"They are in the *post-mortem*[11] room, sir."

11. des autopsies

"Just pack one of them in antiseptics and give it to Dr Hardacre."

And so I found myself back at Rodenhurst before dinner with this curious outcome[12] of my day in town. I still said nothing to Sir Dominick, but I

12. conclusion

slept that night in the laboratory, and I placed the lascar's hand in one of the glass jars at the end of my couch.

So interested was I in the result of my experiment that sleep was out of the question. I sat with a shaded lamp beside me and waited patiently for my visitor. This time I saw him clearly from the first[1]. He appeared beside the door, nebulous for an instant, and then hardening into as distinct an outline[2] as any living man. The slippers[3] beneath his grey gown were red and heelless[4], which accounted for[5] the low, shuffling sound which he made as he walked. As on the previous night he passed slowly along the line of bottles[6] until he paused before that which contained the hand. He reached up to it[7], his whole figure quivering with expectation[8], took it down, examined it eagerly[9], and then, with a face which was convulsed with fury and disappointment, he hurled it down[10] on the floor. There was a crash which resounded throughout the house, and when I looked up the mutilated Indian had disappeared. A moment later my door flew open and Sir Dominick rushed in.

"You are not hurt?" he cried.

"No—but deeply disappointed."

He looked in astonishment at the splinters[11] of glass, and the brown hand lying upon the floor.

"Good God!" he cried. "What is this?"

I told him my idea and its wretched sequel[12]. He listened intently, but shook his head.

"It was well thought of," said he, "but I fear that there is no such easy end to my sufferings. But one thing I now insist upon. It is that you shall never again upon any pretext occupy this

1. dès le début
2. se détachant aussi nettement
3. pantoufles
4. sans talon
5. expliquait
6. bocaux
7. leva le bras pour l'atteindre
8. le corps tremblant d'impatience
9. intensément
10. le lança à toute volée
11. bris
12. malheureuse suite

room. My fears that something might have happened to you—when I heard that crash—have been the most acute of all the agonies[1] which I have undergone. I will not expose myself to a repetition of it."

He allowed me, however, to spend the remainder of the night where I was, and I lay there worrying over the problem and lamenting my own failure[2]. With the first light of morning there was the Lascar's hand still lying upon the floor to remind me of my fiasco. I lay looking at it—and as I lay suddenly an idea flew like a bullet through my head and brought me quivering with excitement out of my couch. I raised the grim relic[3] from where it had fallen. Yes, it was indeed so. The hand was the *left* hand of the Lascar.

By the first train I was on my way to town, and hurried at once to the Seamen's Hospital. I remembered that both hands of the Lascar had been amputated, but I was terrified lest[4] the precious organ which I was in search of might have been already consumed in the crematory. My suspense[5] was soon ended. It had still been preserved in the *post-mortem* room. And so I returned to Rodenhurst in the evening with my mission accomplished and the material for a fresh experiment.

But Sir Dominick Holden would not hear of[6] my occupying[7] the laboratory again. To all my entreaties[8] he turned a deaf ear[9]. It offended his sense of hospitality, and he could no longer permit it. I left the hand, therefore[10], as I had done its fellow[11] the night before, and I occupied a comfortable bedroom in another portion of the house, some distance from the scene of my adventures.

1. douleurs
2. d'avoir échoué
3. triste vestige
4. craignais fort que
5. appréhension
6. refusa
7. que j'occupasse
8. mes demandes pressantes,
9. fit la sourde oreille
10. par conséquent
11. comme j'avais laissé l'autre

But in spite of that my sleep was not destined to be uninterrupted. In the dead of night[1] my host burst into my room, a lamp in his hand. His huge, gaunt figure[2] was enveloped in a loose dressing-gown[3], and his whole appearance might certainly have seemed more formidable[4] to a weak-nerved[5] man than that of the Indian of the night before. But it was not his entrance so much as[6] his expression which amazed me. He had turned suddenly younger by twenty years at the least[7]. His eyes were shining, his features radiant, and he waved one hand in triumph over his head. I sat up astounded, staring sleepily at this extraordinary visitor. But his words soon drove[8] the sleep from my eyes.

"We have done it! We have succeeded!" he shouted. "My dear Hardacre, how can I ever in this world repay you?"

"You don't mean to say that it is all right?"

"Indeed I do. I was sure that you would not mind being awakened to hear such blessed news[9]."

"Mind! I should think not indeed. But is it really certain?"

"I have no doubt whatever upon the point. I owe you such a debt, my dear nephew, as I have never owed a man before, and never expected to. What can I possibly do for you that is commensurate[10]? Providence must have sent you to my rescue. You have saved both my reason and my life, for another six months of this must have seen me either in a cell or a coffin[11]. And my wife—it was wearing her out[12] before my eyes. Never could I have believed that any human being could have

1. En pleine nuit,
2. haute taille décharnée
3. peignoir lâche
4. impressionnante
5. trop nerveux
6. ce fut plutôt
7. avait rajeuni d'au moins 20 ans
8. chassèrent
9. merveilleuse nouvelle
10. qui soit à la hauteur
11. à n'en pas douter, m'aurait fait enfermer ou mettre en terre
12. sapait ses forces

lifted this burden off me." He seized my hand and wrung it in his bony grip[1].

"It was only an experiment—a forlorn hope[2]—but I am delighted from my heart[3] that it has succeeded. But how do you know that it is all right? Have you seen something?"

He seated himself at the foot of my bed.

"I have seen enough," said he. "It satisfies me[4] that I shall be troubled no more. What has passed is easily told. You know that at a certain hour this creature always comes to me. Tonight he arrived at the usual time, and aroused me with even more violence than is his custom[5]. I can only surmise[6] that his disappointment of last night increased the bitterness of his anger[7] against me. He looked angrily at me, and then went on his usual round. But in a few minutes I saw him, for the fist time since this persecution began, return to my chamber. He was smiling. I saw the gleam of his white teeth through the dim light. He stood facing me at the end of my bed, and three times he made the low Eastern salaam[8] which is their solemn leave-taking[9]. And the third time that he bowed[10] he raised his arms over his head, and I saw his *two* hands outstretched in the air. So he vanished, and, as I believe, for ever."

So that is the curious experience which won me the affection and the gratitude of my celebrated uncle, the famous Indian surgeon. His anticipations were realised, and never again was he disturbed by the visits of the restless[11] hillman in search of his lost member. Sir Dominick and Lady Holden spent a very happy old age, unclouded[12], so far as I know, by[13] any trouble, and they finally died during the great influenza epidemic[14] within

1. de sa poigne osseuse
2. dernier espoir
3. profondément
4. me donne la certitude
5. qu'à son habitude
6. ne puis que supposer
7. sa furieuse rancœur
8. profond salut oriental
9. formule d'adieu
10. au troisième salut,
11. sans repos
12. libre
13. de
14. épidémie de grippe

a few weeks of each other. In his lifetime he always turned to me for advice in everything which concerned that English life of which he knew so little; and I aided him also in the purchase[1] and development[2] of his estates. It was no great surprise to me, therefore, that I found myself eventually promoted over the heads[3] of five exasperated cousins, and changed in a single day from a hard-working country doctor into the head[4] of an important Wiltshire family. I, at least, have reason to bless the memory of the man with the brown hand, and the day when I was fortunate enough to relieve[5] Rodenhurst of his unwelcome presence.

1. achat
2. la mise en valeur
3. qu'on me donnât finalement la préférence, aux dépens
4. à chef
5. débarrasser

THE RING OF THOTH

by Arthur Conan Doyle

Mr John Vansittart Smith, FRS[1], of 147A Gower Street, was a man whose energy of purpose[2] and clearness of thought might have placed him in the very first rank[3] of scientific observers. He was the victim, however, of a universal ambition which prompted him to aim at[4] distinction in many subjects rather than preeminence in one. In his early days[5] he had shown an aptitude for zoology and for botany which caused his friends to look upon him as a second Darwin, but when a professorship[6] was almost within his reach he had suddenly discontinued[7] his studies and turned his whole attention to chemistry. Here his researches upon the spectra of the metals had won him his fellowship in[8] the Royal Society; but again he played the coquette with his subject, and after a year's absence from the laboratory he joined the Oriental Society, and delivered a paper[9] on the Hieroglyphic and Demotic inscriptions of El Kab, thus giving a crowning example both of the versatility[10] and of the inconstancy of his talents.

The most fickle[11] of wooers[12], however, is apt to be caught at last[13], and so it was with John Vansittart Smith. The more he burrowed his way into[14] Egyptology the more impressed he became

1. [Fellow of the Royal Society]
2. la détermination énergique
3. parmi l'élite
4. viser
5. jeunesse,
6. poste de professeur universitaire
7. interrompu
8. nomination en tant que membre de
9. article
10. polyvalence
11. inconstant
12. des soupirants
13. peut finir par se faire prendre
14. creusait

by the vast field which it opened to the inquirer[1], and by the extreme importance of a subject which promised to throw a light upon the first germs of human civilisation and the origin of the greater part of our arts and sciences. So struck was Mr. Smith that he straightway[2] married an Egyptological young lady who had written upon the sixth dynasty, and having thus secured[3] a sound[4] base of operations he set himself to collect materials for a work which should unite the research of Lepsius[5] and the ingenuity of Champollion. The preparation of this *magnum opus*[6] entailed[7] many hurried visits to the magnificent Egyptian collections of the Louvre, upon the last of which, no longer ago than the middle of last October, he became involved in a most strange and noteworthy[8] adventure.

The trains had been slow and the Channel had been rough, so that the student arrived in Paris in a somewhat befogged and feverish condition[9]. On reaching the Hôtel de France, in the Rue Laffitte, he had thrown himself upon a sofa for a couple of hours, but finding that he was unable to sleep, he determined, in spite of his fatigue, to make his way to the Louvre, settle[10] the point which he had come to decide, and take the evening train back to Dieppe. Having come to this conclusion, he donned[11] his greatcoat, for[12] it was a raw rainy[13] day, and made his way across the Boulevard des Italiens and down the Avenue de l'Opéra. Once in the Louvre he was on familiar ground, and he speedily made his way to the collection of papyri which it was his intention to consult.

The warmest admirers of John Vansittart Smith could hardly claim for him that he was[14] a hand-

1. chercheur
2. immédiatement
3. s'étant ainsi assuré d'
4. solide
5. [égyptologue allemand, postérieur à Champollion]
6. grand œuvre [latin]
7. impliquait
8. remarquable
9. l'esprit embrumé et quelque peu fiévreux
10. trancher
11. enfila
12. car
13. froid et pluvieux
14. le faire passer pour

some man. His high-beaked[1] nose and prominent chin had something of the same acute and incisive character which distinguished his intellect. He held his head in a birdlike fashion[2], and birdlike, too, was the pecking motion[3] with which, in conversation, he threw out his objections and retorts. As he stood, with the high collar of his greatcoat raised to his ears, he might have seen from the reflection in the glass-case before him that his appearance was a singular one. Yet it came upon him as a sudden jar[4] when an English voice behind him exclaimed in very audible tones, "What a queer-looking mortal!"

The student had a large amount of petty vanity in his composition which manifested itself by an ostentatious and overdone disregard[5] of all personal considerations. He straightened his lips and looked rigidly at the roll of papyrus, while his heart filled with bitterness against the whole race of travelling Britons[6].

"Yes," said another voice, "he really is an extraordinary fellow."

"Do you know," said the first speaker, "one could almost believe that by the continual contemplation of mummies[7] the chap has become half a mummy himself?"

"He has certainly an Egyptian cast of countenance[8]," said the other.

John Vansittart Smith spun round upon his heel with the intention of shaming[9] his countrymen by a corrosive remark or two. To his surprise and relief, the two young fellows who had been conversing had their shoulders turned towards him, and were gazing at one of the Louvre

1. aquilin

2. à la façon d'un oiseau

3. l'air de béqueter

4. irritation

5. mépris exagéré

6. l'ensemble des Britanniques en voyage

7. momies,

8. des traits égyptiens

9. faire honte à

1. employés
2. partirent à pas bruyants
3. bavards
4. apercevoir
5. sursauta
6. visage
7. front large
8. teint sombre
9. sarcophages
10. ne pouvait être
11. s'approcha doucement
12. à l'aise
13. juste milieu
14. brusquerie
15. jovialité d'un égal
16. profil
17. surnaturel
18. Aux tempes et sur les pommettes,

attendants[1] who was polishing some brass-work at the other side of the room.

"Carter will be waiting for us at the Palais Royal," said one tourist to the other, glancing at his watch, and they clattered away[2], leaving the student to his labours.

"I wonder what these chatterers[3] call an Egyptian cast of countenance," thought John Vansittart Smith, and he moved his position slightly in order to catch a glimpse of[4] the man's face. He started[5] as his eyes fell upon it. It was indeed the very face[6] with which his studies had made him familiar. The regular statuesque features, broad brow[7], well-rounded chin, and dusky complexion[8] were the exact counterpart of the innumerable statues, mummy-cases[9], and pictures which adorned the walls of the apartment. The thing was beyond all[10] coincidence. The man must be an Egyptian. The national angularity of the shoulders and narrowness of the hips were alone sufficient to identify him.

John Vansittart Smith shuffled towards[11] the attendant with some intention of addressing him. He was not light of touch[12] in conversation, and found it difficult to strike the happy mean[13] between the brusqueness[14] of the superior and the geniality of the equal[15]. As he came nearer, the man presented his side face[16] to him, but kept his gaze still bent upon his work. Vansittart Smith, fixing his eyes upon the fellow's skin, was conscious of a sudden impression that there was something inhuman and preternatural[17] about its appearance. Over the temple and cheek-bone[18] it was as glazed and as shiny as varnished parchment. There was no suggestion of pores. One could not fancy[1] a drop of moisture[2] upon that arid surface. From brow to chin, however, it was cross-hatched by[3] a million delicate wrinkles[4], which shot and interlaced as though Nature in some Maori mood had tried how wild and intricate a pattern she could devise[5].

"*Où est la collection de Memphis?*" asked the student, with the awkward[6] air of a man who is devising[7] a question merely for the purpose of[8] opening a conversation.

"*C'est là,*" replied the man brusquely, nodding his head at the other side of the room.

"*Vous êtes un Égyptien, n'est-ce pas?*" asked the Englishman.

The attendant looked up and turned his strange dark eyes upon his questioner. They were vitreous, with a misty dry shininess, such as Smith had never seen in a human head before. As he gazed into them he saw some strong emotion gather in their depths, which rose and deepened until it broke into a look of something akin both to horror and to hatred[9].

"*Non, monsieur : je suis français.*" The man turned abruptly and bent low over his polishing. The student gazed at him for a moment in astonishment, and then turning to a chair in a retired corner behind one of the doors he proceeded to make notes of his researches among the papyri. His thoughts, however, refused to return into their natural groove[10]. They would run upon[11] the enigmatical attendant with the sphinx-like face and the parchment skin.

"Where have I seen such eyes?" said Vansittart Smith to himself. "There is something saurian about them, something reptilian. There's the

1. Impossible d'imaginer
2. une goutte de sueur
3. zébré d'
4. fines rides
5. s'était essayé à son motif le plus dense et extravagant
6. gauche
7. forge
8. uniquement pour
9. proche de l'horreur et de la haine
10. reprendre leur cours naturel
11. ne roulaient que sur

membrana nictitans[1] of the snakes," he mused[2], bethinking himself of[3] his zoological studies. "It gives a shiny effect. But there was something more here. There was a sense of power, of wisdom[4]—so I read them—and of weariness, utter weariness[5], and ineffable despair. It may be all imagination, but I never had so strong an impression. By Jove, I must have another look at them!" He rose and paced round the Egyptian rooms, but the man who had excited his curiosity had disappeared.

The student sat down again in his quiet corner, and continued to work at his notes. He had gained the information which he required from the papyri, and it only remained to write it down while it was still fresh in his memory. For a time his pencil travelled rapidly over the paper, but soon the lines became less level[6], the words more blurred[7], and finally the pencil tinkled down upon the floor[8], and the head of the student dropped heavily forward upon his chest. Tired out[9] by his journey[10], he slept so soundly in his lonely post behind the door that neither the clanking civil guard, nor the footsteps of sightseers[11], nor even the loud hoarse bell[12] which gives the signal for closing, were sufficient to arouse him.

Twilight deepened into darkness, the bustle[13] from the Rue de Rivoli waxed[14] and then waned[15], distant Notre-Dame clanged out[16] the hour of midnight, and still the dark and lonely figure[17] sat silently in the shadow. It was not until close upon one in the morning[18] that, with a sudden gasp and an intaking of the breath[19], Vansittart Smith returned to consciousness. For a moment it flashed upon him that he had dropped asleep in

1. troisième paupière [latin]
2. songea-t-il
3. se remémorant
4. sagesse
5. pure lassitude
6. moins droites
7. se brouillèrent
8. tintinnabula en tombant à terre
9. Épuisé
10. voyage
11. pas des visiteurs
12. forte sirène
13. agitation
14. augmenta
15. faiblit
16. sonna
17. silhouette solitaire
18. avant presque une heure du matin
19. inspiration et un hoquet soudains

his study-chair at home. The moon was shining fitfully[1] through the unshuttered window, however, and, as his eye ran along the lines of mummies and the endless array[2] of polished cases, he remembered clearly where he was and how he came there. The student was not a nervous man. He possessed that love of a novel[3] situation which is peculiar to his race[4]. Stretching out his cramped limbs[5], he looked at his watch, and burst into a chuckle[6] as he observed the hour. The episode would make an admirable anecdote to be introduced into his next paper as a relief to the graver and heavier speculations[7]. He was a little cold, but wide awake and much refreshed. It was no wonder that the guardians had overlooked him, for the door threw its heavy black shadow right across him.

The complete silence was impressive. Neither outside nor inside was there a creak or a murmur. He was alone with the dead men of a dead civilisation. What though the outer city reeked of the garish[8] nineteenth century! In all this chamber there was scarce[9] an article, from the shrivelled ear of wheat[10] to the pigment-box of the painter, which had not held its own against[11] four thousand years. Here was the flotsam and jetsam washed up[12] by the great ocean of time from that far-off[13] empire. From stately[14] Thebes, from lordly[15] Luxor, from the great temples of Heliopolis, from a hundred rifled[16] tombs, these relics had been brought. The student glanced round at the long silent figures who flickered vaguely up through the gloom, at the busy toilers[17] who were now so restful, and he fell into a reverent and thoughtful mood. An unwonted[18] sense

1. par intermittence
2. alignement
3. inédite
4. typique de ce genre d'hommes
5. Étirant ses membres engourdis
6. d'un petit rire
7. hypothèses
8. On percevait pourtant, au-dehors, les effluves du clinquant
9. il était difficile de trouver
10. de l'épi de blé desséché
11. qui n'ait pas tenu
12. le rebut laissé
13. lointain
14. l'altière
15. la noble
16. fouillées
17. acteurs d'un labeur incessant
18. rare

of his own youth and insignificance came over him. Leaning back in his chair, he gazed dreamily down the long vista of rooms, all silvery with the moonshine, which extend through the whole wing of the widespread building. His eyes fell upon the yellow glare of a distant lamp.

John Vansittart Smith sat up[1] on his chair with his nerves all on edge[2]. The light was advancing slowly towards him, pausing from time to time, and then coming jerkily onwards[3]. The bearer moved noiselessly. In the utter[4] silence there was no suspicion of the pat of a footfall[5]. An idea of robbers entered the Englishman's head. He snuggled up further into the corner[6]. The light was two rooms off[7]. Now it was in the next chamber, and still there was no sound. With something approaching to a thrill of fear the student observed a face, floating in the air as it were[8], behind the flare of the lamp. The figure was wrapped in shadow, but the light fell full upon the strange eager[9] face. There was no mistaking[10] the metallic glistening eyes and the cadaverous skin. It was the attendant with whom he had conversed.

Vansittart Smith's first impulse was to come forward and address him[11]. A few words of explanation would set the matter clear, and lead doubtless to his being conducted to some side door from which he might make his way to his hotel. As the man entered the chamber, however, there was something so stealthy[12] in his movements, and so furtive in his expression, that the Englishman altered his intention. This was clearly no ordinary official walking the rounds[13]. The fellow wore felt-soled[14] slippers, stepped with a rising chest[15], and glanced quickly from left to right,

1. se redressa
2. les nerfs à vif
3. avançant par à-coups
4. parfait
5. pas l'ombre d'un pas feutré
6. se rencogna
7. plus loin
8. pour ainsi dire
9. ardent
10. Impossible de se méprendre sur
11. pour lui adresser la parole
12. si furtif
13. faisant sa ronde
14. à semelles de feutre
15. avança en redressant le torse

while his hurried gasping breathing[1] thrilled[2] the flame of his lamp. Vansittart Smith crouched silently back[3] into the corner and watched him keenly[4], convinced that his errand was one of secret and probably sinister import[5].

There was no hesitation in the other's movements. He stepped lightly and swiftly across to one of the great cases, and, drawing a key from his pocket, he unlocked it. From the upper shelf he pulled down a mummy, which he bore away with him[6], and laid it with much care and solicitude upon the ground. By it[7] he placed his lamp, and then squatting down beside it in Eastern fashion[8] he began with long quivering fingers to undo the cerecloths[9] and bandages which girt it round. As the crackling rolls of linen peeled off[10] one after the other, a strong aromatic odour filled the chamber, and fragments of scented wood and of spices pattered down[11] upon the marble floor.

It was clear to John Vansittart Smith that this mummy had never been unswathed[12] before. The operation interested him keenly. He thrilled all over with curiosity, and his birdlike head protruded further and further from behind the door. When, however, the last roll had been removed from the four-thousand-year-old head, it was all that he could do[13] to stifle[14] an outcry of amazement[15]. First, a cascade of long, black, glossy tresses poured over the workman's hands and arms. A second turn of the bandage revealed a low, white forehead, with a pair of delicately arched eyebrows[16]. A third uncovered a pair of bright, deeply fringed eyes, and a straight, well-cut nose, while a fourth and last showed a sweet, full, sensitive mouth, and a beautifully curved

1. halètement précipité
2. faisait trembler
3. retourna s'accroupir
4. avec intensité
5. qu'il venait accomplir de secrets et mauvais desseins
6. emporta
7. À côté de la momie
8. à l'orientale
9. bandelettes mortuaires
10. partirent
11. tombèrent en s'effritant
12. défaite de ses bandelettes
13. il eut du mal
14. à réprimer
15. un cri de surprise
16. sourcils finement arqués

chin. The whole face was one of extraordinary loveliness, save for[1] the one blemish that[2] in the centre of the forehead there was a single irregular, coffee-coloured splotch[3]. It was a triumph of the embalmer's art. Vansittart Smith's eyes grew larger and larger as he gazed upon it, and he chirruped in his throat with[4] satisfaction.

Its effect upon the Egyptologist was as nothing[5], however, compared with that which it produced upon[6] the strange attendant. He threw his hands up into the air, burst into a harsh clatter of words, and then, hurling himself down upon the ground[7] beside the mummy, he threw his arms round her, and kissed her repeatedly upon the lips and brow. "*Ma petite!*" he groaned in French. "*Ma pauvre petite!*" His voice broke with emotion, and his innumerable wrinkles[8] quivered and writhed[9], but the student observed in the lamplight that his shining eyes were still as dry and tearless as two beads of steel. For some minutes he lay, with a twitching face, crooning and moaning[10] over the beautiful head. Then he broke into a sudden smile[11], said some words in an unknown tongue, and sprang to his feet with the vigorous air of one who has braced himself[12] for an effort.

In the centre of the room there was a large circular case which contained, as the student had frequently remarked, a magnificent collection of early Egyptian rings and precious stones. To this the attendant strode[13], and, unlocking it, he threw it open. On the ledge at the side[14] he placed his lamp, and beside it a small earthenware jar[15] which he had drawn from his pocket. He then took a handful of rings from the case, and with a most serious and anxious face he pro-

1. hormis
2. un unique défaut :
3. tache brune
4. eut un gargouillis de
5. nul
6. à l'effet produit sur
7. se jetant à terre
8. rides
9. se tordirent
10. parlant d'une voix douce ou gémissante
11. se mit à sourire
12. s'est armé de courage
13. L'employé s'en approcha à grands pas
14. rebord
15. pot en terre

ceeded to smear each in turn with some[1] liquid substance from the earthen pot, holding them to the light as he did so. He was clearly disappointed with the first lot, for[2] he threw them petulantly[3] back into the case, and drew out some more. One of these, a massive ring with a large crystal set in it[4], he seized and eagerly[5] tested with the contents[6] of the jar. Instantly he uttered[7] a cry of joy, and threw out his arms in a wild gesture which upset[8] the pot and sent the liquid streaming across the floor to the very feet[9] of the Englishman. The attendant drew a red handkerchief from his bosom, and, mopping up the mess[10], he followed it into the corner, where in a moment he found himself face to face with his observer.

"Excuse me," said John Vansittart Smith, with all imaginable politeness; "I have been unfortunate enough to fall asleep behind this door."

"And you have been watching me?" the other asked in English, with a most venomous look on his corpse-like[11] face.

The student was a man of veracity. "I confess," said he, "that I have noticed your movements, and that they have aroused my curiosity and interest in the highest degree."

The man drew a long flamboyant-bladed knife from his bosom. "You have had a very narrow escape[12]," he said; "had I seen you[13] ten minutes ago, I should have driven this through your heart[14]. As it is[15], if you touch me or interfere with me in any way you are a dead man."

"I have no wish to interfere with you," the student answered. "My presence here is entirely accidental. All I ask is that you will have the extreme kindness to show me out[16] through some side

1. recouvrir chacune [des bagues] d'une
2. car
3. avec emportement
4. incrusté
5. vivement
6. contenu
7. lança
8. renversa
9. jusqu'aux pieds
10. en épongeant le liquide
11. cadavérique
12. l'avez échappé belle
13. si je vous avais vu
14. vous aurais enfoncé cela dans le cœur
15. À présent
16. de me montrer la sortie

door." He spoke with great suavity, for the man was still pressing the tip of his dagger[1] against the palm of his left hand, as though to assure himself of its sharpness, while his face preserved its malignant expression.

1. la pointe de sa dague

"If I thought?" said he. "But no, perhaps it is as well. What is your name?"

The Englishman gave it.

"Vansittart Smith," the other repeated. "Are you the same Vansittart Smith who gave a paper in London upon El Kab? I saw a report of it. Your knowledge of the subject is contemptible[2]."

2. méprisable

"Sir!" cried the Egyptologist.

"Yet[3] it is superior to that of many who make even greater pretensions. The whole keystone[4] of our old life in Egypt was not the inscriptions or monuments of which you make so much, but was our hermetic philosophy and mystic knowledge[5], of which you say little or nothing."

3. Pourtant,
4. clef de voûte
5. savoir

"Our old life!" repeated the scholar[6], wide-eyed; and then suddenly, "Good God, look at the mummy's face!"

6. savant

The strange man turned and flashed his light upon the dead woman, uttering a long doleful cry[7] as he did so. The action of the air had already undone all the art of the embalmer. The skin had fallen away, the eyes had sunk inwards[8], the discoloured lips had writhed away[9] from the yellow teeth, and the brown mark upon the forehead alone[10] showed that it was indeed the same face which had shown such youth and beauty a few short minutes before.

7. lançant un grand cri de douleur
8. rentrés
9. s'étaient écartées
10. seule la tache brune du front

The man flapped his hands together in grief and horror. Then mastering himself by a strong effort he turned his hard eyes once more upon the Englishman.

"It does not matter," he said, in a shaking voice. "It does not really matter. I came here tonight with the fixed determination to do something. It is now done. All else is as nothing. I have found my quest[1]. The old curse[2] is broken. I can rejoin her. What matter about her inanimate shell so long as her spirit is awaiting me at the other side of the veil!"

"These are wild words," said Vansittart Smith. He was becoming more and more convinced that he had to do with a madman.

"Time presses, and I must go," continued the other. "The moment is at hand[3] for which I have waited this weary time. But I must show you out first[4]. Come with me."

Taking up the lamp, he turned from the disordered chamber, and led the student swiftly through the long series of the Egyptian, Assyrian, and Persian apartments. At the end of the latter he pushed open a small door let into the wall and descended a winding[5] stone stair. The Englishman felt the cold fresh air of the night upon his brow. There was a door opposite him which appeared to communicate with the street. To the right of this another door stood ajar[6], throwing a spurt[7] of yellow light across the passage. "Come in here!" said the attendant shortly.

Vansittart Smith hesitated. He had hoped that he had come to the end of his adventure. Yet his curiosity was strong within him. He could not leave the matter unsolved, so he followed his strange companion into the lighted chamber.

1. Ma quête est à son terme
2. maléfice
3. proche
4. d'abord vous montrer la sortie
5. en colimaçon
6. était entrouverte
7. rai

It was a small room, such as is devoted to a *concierge.* A wood fire sparkled in the grate[1]. At one side stood a truckle bed[2], and at the other a coarse[3] wooden chair, with a round table in the centre, which bore the remains of a meal. As the visitor's eye glanced round he could not but[4] remark with an ever-recurring thrill[5] that all the small details of the room were of the most quaint[6] design and antique workmanship[7]. The candlesticks, the vases upon the chimney-piece, the fire-irons[8], the ornaments upon the walls, were all such as he had been wont[9] to associate with the remote[10] past. The gnarled[11] heavy-eyed man sat himself down upon the edge[12] of the bed, and motioned his guest into the chair.

"There may be design in this," he said, still speaking excellent English. "It may be decreed that I should leave some account behind as a warning to[13] all rash mortals who would set their wits up against[14] workings of Nature. I leave it with you[15]. Make such use as you will of it[16]. I speak to you now with my feet upon the threshold[17] of the other world.

"I am, as you surmised[18], an Egyptian—not one of the down-trodden[19] race of slaves who now inhabit the Delta of the Nile, but a survivor of that fiercer and harder people who tamed[20] the Hebrew, drove the Ethiopian back into the southern deserts, and built those mighty works[21] which have been the envy and the wonder of all after generations[22]. It was in the reign of Tuthmosis, sixteen hundred years before the birth of Christ, that I first saw the light. You shrink away[23] from me. Wait, and you will see that I am more to be pitied than to be feared.

1. âtre
2. lit gigogne
3. rustique
4. que
5. nouveau frisson
6. suranné
7. facture ancienne
8. pique-feux
9. avait coutume
10. lointain
11. revêche
12. au bord
13. doive laisser un récit avertissant
14. opposeraient leur intelligence aux
15. vous laisse juge
16. Faites-en l'usage que vous voudrez
17. au seuil
18. l'avez supposé
19. opprimée
20. dompta
21. œuvres puissantes
22. des générations suivantes
23. vous écartez

"My name was Sosra. My father had been the chief priest of Osiris in the great temple of Abaris, which stood in those days upon the Bubastic branch of the Nile. I was brought up in the temple and was trained in all those mystic arts which are spoken of in your own Bible. I was an apt pupil[1]. Before I was sixteen I had learned all which the wisest priest could teach me. From that time on[2] I studied Nature's secrets for myself, and shared my knowledge with no man.

"Of all the questions which attracted me there were none over which I laboured so long as over those which concern themselves with the nature of life. I probed deeply into[3] the vital principle. The aim[4] of medicine had been to drive away disease[5] when it appeared. It seemed to me that a method might be devised[6] which should so fortify the body as to prevent weakness[7] or death from ever taking hold of it[8]. It is useless that I should recount[9] my researches. You would scarce comprehend them if I did. They were carried out partly upon animals, partly upon slaves, and partly on myself. Suffice it[10] that their result was to furnish me with a substance which, when injected into the blood, would endow the body with strength[11] to resist the effects of time, of violence, or of disease. It would not indeed confer immortality, but its potency would endure for[12] many thousands of years. I used it upon a cat, and afterwards drugged the creature with the most deadly poisons. That cat is alive in Lower Egypt at the present moment. There was nothing of mystery or magic in the matter. It was simply a chemical discovery, which may well be made again.

1. élève capable
2. Dès lors,
3. sondai profondément
4. but
5. repousser la maladie
6. élaborée
7. empêcher que la faiblesse
8. s'en emparent
9. je narre
10. Sachez seulement
11. dotait le corps de la force
12. durerait

"Love of life runs high in[1] the young. It seemed to me that I had broken away from all human care now that I had abolished pain and driven death to such a distance. With a light heart I poured the accursed stuff into my veins. Then I looked round for some one whom I could benefit. There was a young priest of Thoth, Parmes by name[2], who had won my goodwill[3] by his earnest[4] nature and his devotion[5] to his studies. To him I whispered my secret, and at his request I injected him with my elixir. I should now, I reflected, never be without a companion of the same age as myself.

"After this grand discovery I relaxed my studies to some extent, but Parmes continued his[6] with redoubled energy. Every day I could see him working with his flasks and his distiller in the Temple of Thoth, but he said little to me as to the result of his labours. For my own part, I used to walk through the city and look around me with exultation as I reflected that all this was destined to pass away, and that only I should remain. The people would bow to me[7] as they passed me, for the fame of my knowledge had gone abroad.

"There was war at this time, and the Great King had sent down his soldiers to the eastern boundary to drive away the Hyksos[8]. A Governor, too, was sent to Abaris, that he might hold it for the[9] King. I had heard much of the beauty of the daughter of this Governor, but one day as I walked out with Parmes we met her, borne upon the shoulders of her slaves. I was struck with love as with lightning[10]. My heart went out from me[11]. I could have thrown myself beneath the feet of her bearers[12]. This was my woman. Life without her was impossible. I swore by the head of Horus

1. est très puissant chez
2. nommé Parmes
3. amitié
4. sérieuse
5. zèle
6. les siennes
7. me saluaient
8. [populations du Proche-Orient d'où sortit la 15e dynastie égyptienne]
9. afin de la défendre au nom du
10. par la foudre
11. ne m'appartint plus
12. porteurs

that she should be mine. I swore it to the Priest of Thoth. He turned away from me with a brow which was as black as midnight[1].

"There is no need to tell you of our wooing[2]. She came to love me even as[3] I loved her. I learned that Parmes had seen her before I did, and had shown her that he too loved her, but I could smile at his passion, for I knew that her heart was mine. The white plague[4] had come upon the city and many were stricken, but I laid my hands upon the sick and nursed them[5] without fear or scathe[6]. She marvelled at my daring[7]. Then I told her my secret, and begged her that she would let me use my art upon her.

"'Your flower shall then be unwithered[8], Atma,' I said. 'Other things may pass away, but you and I, and our great love for each other, shall outlive the tomb of King Chefru.'

"But she was full of timid, maidenly[9] objections. 'Was it right?' she asked, 'was it not a thwarting of the will[10] of the gods? If the great Osiris had wished that our years should be so long, would he not himself have brought it about[11]?'

"With fond and loving words I overcame her doubts, and yet she hesitated. It was a great question, she said. She would think it over[12] for this one night[13]. In the morning I should know[14] her resolution. Surely one night was not too much to ask. She wished to pray to Isis for help in her decision.

"With a sinking heart[15] and a sad foreboding of evil[16] I left her with her tirewomen[17]. In the morning, when the early sacrifice was over, I hurried to her house. A frightened slave met me upon the steps. Her mistress was ill, she said, very ill.

1. l'air furieux
2. nos amours
3. autant que
4. peste
5. les soignai
6. ni dommage
7. audace
8. ainsi ne se flétrira pas
9. de jeune fille
10. se soustraire à la volonté
11. fait en sorte que ce soit le cas
12. y réfléchirait encore
13. juste cette nuit
14. connaîtrais
15. Le cœur lourd
16. triste pressentiment,
17. ses femmes

In a frenzy I broke my way through the attendants, and rushed through hall and corridor to my Atma's chamber. She lay upon her couch, her head high upon the pillow, with a pallid face and a glazed eye. On her forehead there blazed a single angry purple patch. I knew that hell-mark[1] of old[2]. It was the scar[3] of the white plague, the sign-manual of death.

1. signe infernal
2. depuis longtemps
3. la marque

"Why should I speak of that terrible time? For months I was mad, fevered, delirious, and yet I could not die. Never did an Arab thirst after the sweet wells as I longed after death. Could poison or steel have shortened the thread[4] of my existence, I should soon have rejoined my love[5] in the land with the narrow portal. I tried, but it was of no avail[6]. The accursed[7] influence was too strong upon me. One night as I lay upon my couch, weak and weary[8], Parmes, the priest of Thoth, came to my chamber. He stood in the circle of the lamplight, and he looked down upon me with eyes which were bright with a mad joy.

4. fil
5. mon aimée
6. en vain
7. maudite
8. las

"'Why did you let the maiden die?' he asked; 'why did you not strengthen her as you strengthened me?'

"'I was too late,' I answered. `But I had forgot. You also loved her. You are my fellow in misfortune. Is it not terrible to think of the centuries which must pass ere[9] we look upon her again? Fools, fools, that we were to take death to be our enemy!'

9. avant que

"'You may say that,' he cried with a wild laugh; 'the words come well from your lips. For me they have no meaning.'

"'What mean you?' I cried, raising myself upon my elbow. 'Surely, friend, this grief has turned your brain[1].' His face was aflame with joy, and he writhed[2] and shook like one who hath a devil[3].

"'Do you know whither[4] I go?' he asked.

"'Nay[5],' I answered, 'I cannot tell.'

"'I go to her,' said he. 'She lies embalmed in the further tomb by the double palm-tree beyond the city wall.'

"'Why do you go there?' I asked.

"'To die!' he shrieked[6], 'to die! I am not bound by earthen fetters[7].'

"'But the elixir is in your blood,' I cried.

"'I can defy it,' said he; 'I have found a stronger principle which will destroy it. It is working in my veins at this moment, and in an hour I shall be a dead man. I shall join her, and you shall remain behind.'

"As I looked upon him I could see that he spoke words of truth. The light in his eye told me that he was indeed beyond the power of the elixir.

"'You will teach me!' I cried.

"'Never!' he answered.

"'I implore you, by the wisdom of Thoth, by the majesty of Anubis!'

"'It is useless,' he said coldly.

"'Then I will find it out,' I cried.

"'You cannot,' he answered; 'it came to me by chance[8]. There is one ingredient which you can never get. Save that which is in the ring of Thoth, none will ever more be made.

"'In the ring of Thoth!' I repeated; 'where then is the ring of Thoth?'

"'That also you shall never know,' he answered. 'You won her love. Who has won in the end? I leave you to your sordid earth life. My chains are

1. atteint ta raison
2. se tordit
3. est possédé
4. où
5. Non
6. s'égosilla-t-il
7. retenu par des liens terrestres
8. hasard

broken. I must go!' He turned upon his heel and fled from the chamber. In the morning came the news that the Priest of Thoth was dead.

"My days after that were spent in study. I must find this subtle poison which was strong enough to **undo**[1] the elixir. From early dawn to midnight I bent over the **test-tube**[2] and the **furnace**[3]. Above all, I collected the papyri and the chemical flasks of the Priest of Thoth. Alas! they taught me little. Here and there some **hint**[4] or **stray**[5] expression would raise hope in my bosom, but no good ever came of it. Still, month after month, I struggled on. When **my heart grew faint**[6] I would make my way to the tomb by the palm-trees. There, standing by the dead **casket**[7] from which the jewel had **been rifled**[8], I would feel her sweet presence, and would whisper to her that I would rejoin her if **mortal wit**[9] could **solve the riddle**[10].

"Parmes had said that his discovery was connected with the ring of Thoth. I had some remembrance of the **trinket**[11]. It was a large and **weighty**[12] circlet, made, not of gold, but of a rarer and heavier metal brought from the mines of Mount Harbal. Platinum, you call it. The ring had, I remembered, a **hollow**[13] crystal set in it, in which some few drops of liquid might be stored. Now, the secret of Parmes could not have to do with the metal alone, for there were many rings of that metal in the Temple. Was it not more likely that he had stored his precious poison within the cavity of the crystal? I had **scarce come**[14] to this conclusion before, in hunting through his papers, I came upon one which told me that it was indeed so, and that there was still some of the liquid unused.

1. annuler les effets de
2. tube à essais
3. fourneau
4. indication
5. occasionnelle
6. je perdais courage,
7. coffre funéraire
8. dépouillé de son joyau
9. l'esprit d'un mortel
10. résoudre l'énigme
11. colifichet
12. lourd
13. creux
14. étais à peine parvenu

"But how to find the ring? It was not upon him when he was stripped for the embalmer. Of that I made sure. Neither was it among his private effects. In vain I searched every room that he had entered, every box, and vase, and chattel[1] that he had owned. I sifted the very sand[2] of the desert in the places where he had been wont to[3] walk; but, do what I would[4], I could come upon no traces of the ring of Thoth. Yet it may be that my labours would have overcome all obstacles had it not been for[5] a new and unlooked-for misfortune.

"A great war had been waged against the Hyksos, and the Captains of the Great King had been cut off in the desert, with all their bowmen[6] and horsemen. The shepherd tribes were upon us like the locusts[7] in a dry year. From the wilderness of Shur to the great bitter lake there was blood by day and fire by night. Abaris was the bulwark[8] of Egypt, but we could not keep the savages back. The city fell. The Governor and the soldiers were put to the sword[9], and I, with many more, was led away into captivity.

"For years and years I tended cattle[10] in the great plains by the Euphrates. My master died, and his son grew old, but I was still as far from death as ever. At last I escaped upon a swift camel, and made my way back to Egypt. The Hyksos had settled in the land which they had conquered, and their own King ruled over the country. Abaris had been torn down, the city had been burned, and of the great Temple there was nothing left save an unsightly mound[11]. Everywhere the tombs had been rifled[12] and the monuments destroyed. Of my Atma's grave no sign was left. It was buried in the sands of the desert, and the

1. bien meuble
2. tamisai même le sable
3. eu coutume de
4. quoi que je fisse
5. n'eût été
6. archers
7. des sauterelles
8. rempart
9. passés au fil de l'épée
10. gardai le bétail
11. monticule disgracieux
12. mises à sac

palm-trees which marked the spot had long disappeared. The papers of Parmes and the remains of the Temple of Thoth were either destroyed or scattered far and wide over[1] the deserts of Syria. All search after them was vain.

"From that time I gave up all hope of ever finding the ring or discovering the subtle drug. I set myself to live as patiently as might be until the effect of the elixir should wear away[2]. How can you understand how terrible a thing time is, you who have experience only of the narrow course[3] which lies between the cradle[4] and the grave[5]! I know it to my cost[6], I who have floated down the whole stream of history. I was old when Ilium fell. I was very old when Herodotus came to Memphis. I was bowed down with years[7] when the new gospel[8] came upon earth. Yet you see me much as other men are, with the cursed elixir still sweetening my blood, and guarding me against that which I would court[9]. Now at last, at last I have come to the end of it!

"I have travelled in all lands and I have dwelt with all nations. Every tongue is the same to me[10]. I learned them all[11] to help pass the weary time. I need not tell you how slowly they drifted by, the long dawn of modern civilisation, the dreary[12] middle years, the dark times of barbarism. They are all behind me now, I have never looked with the eyes of love upon another woman. Atma knows that I have been constant to her[13].

"It was my custom to read all that the scholars had to say upon Ancient Egypt. I have been in many positions, sometimes affluent[14], sometimes poor, but I have always found enough to enable me to buy the journals which deal with such mat-

1. éparpillés aux quatre vents des
2. s'estompât
3. voie étroite
4. berceau
5. la tombe
6. l'ai appris à mes dépens
7. courbé par les ans
8. évangile
9. me préservant de ce que je voulais conquérir
10. Je ne fais pas de différence entre les langues
11. les ai toutes apprises
12. mornes
13. lui ai été fidèle
14. riche

ters. Some nine months ago I was in San Francisco, when I read an account[1] of some discoveries made in the neighbourhood of Abaris. My heart leapt into my mouth[2] as I read it. It said that the excavator had busied himself in exploring some tombs recently unearthed. In one there had been found an unopened mummy with an inscription upon the outer case setting forth[3] that it contained the body of the daughter of the Governor of the city in the days of Tuthmosis. It added that on removing the outer case there had been exposed a large platinum ring set with a crystal, which had been laid upon the breast of the embalmed woman. This, then was where Parmes had hid the ring of Thoth. He might well say that it was safe[4], for[5] no Egyptian would ever stain his soul[6] by moving even the outer case[7] of a buried friend.

"That very night[8] I set off from San Francisco, and in a few weeks I found myself once more at Abaris, if a few sand-heaps[9] and crumbling walls[10] may retain the name of the great city. I hurried to the Frenchmen who were digging there and asked them for the ring. They replied that both the ring and the mummy had been sent to the Boulak Museum at Cairo. To Boulak I went, but only to be told that Mariette Bey[11] had claimed them[12] and had shipped them to the Louvre. I followed them, and there at last, in the Egyptian chamber, I came, after close upon[13] four thousand years, upon the remains of my Atma, and upon the ring for which I had sought so long.

"But how was I to lay hands upon them? How was I to have them for my very own[14]? It chanced that the office[15] of attendant was vacant. I went to

1. récit

2. Mon sang ne fit qu'un tour

3. annonçant

4. en sûreté

5. car

6. n'eût souillé son âme

7. sarcophage

8. Le soir même,

9. tas de sable

10. ruines

11. M. Auguste Mariette [égyptologue français (1821-1881)]

12. les avait reclamés

13. près de

14. en prendre possession

15. poste

the Director. I convinced him that I knew much about Egypt. In my eagerness[1] I said too much. He remarked that a Professor's chair[2] would suit me better than a seat in the Conciergerie. I knew more, he said, than he did. It was only by blundering[3], and letting him think that he had over-estimated my knowledge, that I prevailed upon him[4] to let me move the few effects which I have retained into this chamber. It is my first and my last night here.

"Such is my story, Mr Vansittart Smith. I need not say more to a man of your perception. By a strange chance[5] you have this night looked upon the face of the woman whom I loved in those far-off days. There were many rings with crystals in the case, and I had to test for the platinum to be sure of the one which I wanted. A glance at the crystal has shown me that the liquid is indeed within it, and that I shall at last be able to shake off that accursed health[6] which has been worse to me than the foulest disease[7]. I have nothing more to say to you. I have unburdened myself[8]. You may tell my story or you may withhold it[9] at your pleasure[10]. The choice rests with you[11]. I owe you some amends[12], for you have had a narrow escape of your life[13] this night. I was a desperate man, and not to be baulked[14] in my purpose[15]. Had I seen you before the thing was done, I might have put it beyond your power to oppose me or to raise an alarm. This is the door. It leads into the Rue de Rivoli. Good night!"

The Englishman glanced back[16]. For a moment the lean figure[17] of Sosra the Egyptian stood framed in the narrow doorway[18]. The next the

1. enthousiasme
2. poste
3. en commettant des erreurs
4. le convainquis
5. hasard,
6. maudite bonne santé
7. plus terrible des maladies
8. déposé mon fardeau
9. la garder pour vous,
10. guise
11. vous incombe
12. vous dois quelque compensation
13. failli perdre la vie
14. n'allais supporter aucun frein
15. pour atteindre mon but
16. eut un regard en arrière
17. mince silhouette
18. se détacha dans l'étroit encadrement de la porte

door had slammed[1], and the heavy rasping[2] of a bolt[3] broke on the silent night.

It was on the second day after his return to London that Mr John Vansittart Smith saw the following concise narrative in the Paris correspondence of *The Times*:—

> *Curious Occurrence[4] in the Louvre.*—Yesterday morning a strange discovery was made in the principal Egyptian Chamber. The *ouvriers* who are employed to clean out the rooms in the morning found one of the attendants lying dead upon the floor with his arms round one of the mummies. So close was his embrace[5] that it was only with the utmost[6] difficulty that they were separated. One of the cases containing valuable rings had been opened and rifled. The authorities are of opinion that the man was bearing away the mummy with some idea of selling it to a private collector, but that he was struck down in the very act by long-standing[7] disease of the heart. It is said that he was a man of uncertain age and eccentric habits, without any living relations[8] to mourn over[9] his dramatic and untimely[10] end.

1. claqué
2. crissement
3. verrou
4. incident
5. Il la tenait si serrée
6. plus grande
7. vieille
8. parent vivant
9. pour pleurer
10. prématurée

THE MASQUE OF THE RED DEATH

by Edgar Allan Poe

The "Red Death" had long devastated the country. No pestilence[1] had ever been so fatal, or so hideous. Blood was its avatar[2] and its seal[3]—the redness and the horror of blood. There were sharp pains, and sudden dizziness[4], and then profuse bleeding at the pores, with dissolution. The scarlet stains[5] upon the body and especially upon the face of the victim, were the pest ban[6] which shut him out[7] from the aid and from the sympathy of his fellow-men[8]. And the whole seizure[9], progress and termination of the disease, were the incidents of half an hour.

But the Prince Prospero was happy and dauntless[10] and sagacious. When his dominions[11] were half depopulated, he summoned to his presence[12] a thousand hale[13] and light-hearted[14] friends from among the knights and dames of his court, and with these retired to the deep seclusion[15] of one of his castellated[16] abbeys. This was an extensive and magnificent structure, the creation of the prince's own eccentric yet august taste. A strong and lofty[17] wall girdled it in[18]. This wall had gates of iron. The courtiers[19], having entered, brought

1. peste
2. forme actuelle
3. sceau
4. un vertige
5. taches écarlates
6. les stigmates
7. le privaient
8. semblables
9. attaque
10. intrépide
11. domaines
12. convoqua
13. vigoureux
14. joyeux
15. retraite
16. fortifiées
17. haut
18. l'entourait
19. courtisans

furnaces[1] and massy hammers[2] and welded the bolts[3]. They resolved to leave means neither of ingress or egress[4] to the sudden impulses of despair or of frenzy from within. The abbey was amply provisioned. With such precautions the courtiers might bid defiance to[5] contagion. The external world could take care of itself. In the meantime[6] it was folly to grieve[7], or to think. The Prince had provided all the appliances[8] of pleasure. There were buffoons, there were *improvisatori*, there were ballet dancers, there were musicians, there was Beauty, there was wine. All these and security were within. Without[9] was the "Red Death".

It was toward the close[10] of the fifth or sixth month of his seclusion, and while the pestilence raged most furiously abroad, that the Prince Prospero entertained[11] his thousand friends at a masked ball of the most unusual magnificence.

It was a voluptuous scene, that masquerade[12]. But first let me tell of the rooms in which it was held. There were seven—an imperial suite. In many palaces, however, such suites form a long and straight vista[13], while the folding[14] doors slide back nearly to the walls on either hand[15], so that the view of the whole extent is scarcely impeded[16]. Here the case was very different; as might have been expected from the duke's love of the *bizarre*. The apartments were so irregularly disposed that the vision embraced but little[17] more than one at a time. There was a sharp turn at every twenty or thirty yards, and at each turn a novel[18] effect. To the right and left, in the middle of each wall, a tall and narrow Gothic window looked out upon a closed corridor which pursued the windings[19] of the suite. These windows were

1. des fourneaux
2. marteaux
3. soudèrent les verrous
4. bloquer tout accès et toute issue
5. défier la
6. En attendant,
7. pleurer
8. attirail
9. Au dehors
10. fin
11. reçut
12. bal masqué
13. perspective
14. à battants
15. de chaque côté
16. à peine entravée
17. l'on ne pouvait guère en voir
18. inédit
19. suivait les méandres

of stained glass[1] whose color varied in accordance with the prevailing hue[2] of the decorations of the chamber into which it opened. That[3] at the eastern extremity was hung[4], for example, in[5] blue—and vividly blue were its windows. The second chamber was purple in its ornaments and tapestries, and here the panes[6] were purple. The third was green throughout[7], and so were the casements[8]. The fourth was furnished and lighted with orange—the fifth with white—the sixth with violet. The seventh apartment was closely shrouded in[9] black velvet tapestries that hung all over the ceiling and down the walls, falling in heavy folds upon a carpet of the same material and hue. But in this chamber only, the color of the windows failed to correspond with the[10] decorations. The panes here were scarlet—a deep blood color. Now[11] in no one of the seven apartments was there any lamp or candelabrum, amid[12] the profusion of golden ornaments that lay scattered to and fro[13] or depended from the roof[14]. There was no light of any kind emanating from lamp or candle within the suite of chambers. But in the corridors that followed the suite, there stood, opposite to each window, a heavy tripod[15], bearing a brazier of fire, that projected its rays through the tinted glass and so glaringly illumined[16] the room. And thus were produced a multitude of gaudy[17] and fantastic appearances. But in the western or black chamber the effect of the fire-light that streamed upon the dark hangings[18] through the blood-tinted panes, was ghastly[19] in the extreme, and produced so wild a look upon the countenances[20] of those who entered, that there were

1. des vitraux
2. teinte dominante
3. Celle [la chambre] qui était
4. tendue
5. de
6. vitres
7. entièrement verte
8. fenêtres
9. recouvert de
10. n'était pas assortie aux
11. Or
12. parmi
13. éparpillés çà et là
14. suspendus au plafond
15. trépied
16. illuminait vivement
17. tapageuses
18. courait sur les tentures noires
19. lugubre
20. une expression si fantastique sur le visage

few of the company bold enough[1] to set foot within its precincts at all[2].

It was in this apartment, also, that there stood against the western wall, a gigantic clock of ebony[3]. Its pendulum swung to and fro[4] with a dull, heavy, monotonous clang; and when the minute-hand[5] made the circuit of the face[6], and the hour was to be stricken[7], there came from the brazen lungs[8] of the clock a sound which was clear and loud and deep and exceedingly musical, but of so peculiar[9] a note and emphasis that, at each lapse of an hour[10], the musicians of the orchestra were constrained to pause, momentarily, in their performance, to harken to the sound[11]; and thus the waltzers perforce ceased their evolutions[12]; and there was a brief disconcert[13] of the whole gay company; and, while the chimes[14] of the clock yet rang, it was observed that the giddiest grew pale[15], and the more aged and sedate[16] passed their hands over their brows as if in confused reverie or meditation. But when the echoes had fully ceased, a light laughter at once pervaded[17] the assembly; the musicians looked at each other and smiled as if at their own nervousness and folly, and made whispering vows[18], each to the other, that the next chiming of the clock should produce in them no similar emotion; and then, after the lapse of sixty minutes, (which embrace three thousand and six hundred seconds of the time that flies), there came yet another chiming of the clock, and then were the same disconcert and tremulousness[19] and meditation as before.

But, in spite of these things, it was a gay and magnificent revel[20]. The tastes of the duke were

1. suffisamment hardis
2. pour y pénétrer
3. ébène
4. oscillait
5. l'aiguille des minutes
6. avait fait le tour du cadran
7. sonnée
8. poumons de laiton
9. si étrange
10. heure
11. l'écouter
12. les valseurs devaient s'arrêter
13. instant de trouble
14. le carillon
15. les plus enjoués pâlissaient
16. calmes
17. parcourait aussitôt
18. juraient à voix basse
19. frémissement
20. fête

peculiar. He had a fine eye for colors and effects. He disregarded[1] the *decora*[2] of mere fashion. His plans were bold and fiery[3], and his conceptions glowed with barbaric lustre[4]. There are some who would have thought him mad. His followers felt that he was not. It was necessary to hear and see and touch him to be *sure* that he was not.

He had directed, in great part, the moveable embellishments[5] of the seven chambers, upon occasion of this great *fête*; and it was his own guiding taste which had given character to the masqueraders[6]. Be sure they were grotesque. There were much glare[7] and glitter and piquancy and phantasm[8]—much of what has been since seen in *Hernani*[9]. There were arabesque figures with unsuited limbs and appointments[10]. There were delirious fancies such as the madman fashions[11]. There were much of the[12] beautiful, much of the wanton[13], much of the *bizarre*, something of the terrible, and not a little of that which might have excited disgust. To and fro in the seven chambers there stalked[14], in fact, a multitude of dreams. And these—the dreams—writhed in, and about[15], taking hue from the[16] rooms, and causing the wild music of thc orchestra to seem as the echo of their steps. And, anon[17], there strikes the ebony clock which stands in the hall of the velvet[18]. And then, for a moment, all is still[19], and all is silent save[20] the voice of the clock. The dreams are stiff-frozen as they stand[21]. But the echoes of the chime die away—they have endured but[22] an instant—and a light, half-subdued[23] laughter floats after them as they depart. And now again the music swells[24], and the dreams live, and writhe to and fro more merrily than ever, taking hue from the

1. méprisait
2. décorum
3. flamboyants
4. brillaient d'un éclat barbare
5. l'agencement des meubles
6. décidé de l'aspect des déguisements
7. Tout n'était que clinquant
8. fantasmagorie
9. [drame audacieux de Victor Hugo]
10. des membres et des proportions incongrus
11. comme en invente le fou
12. beaucoup de
13. exubérance
14. Allaient et venaient
15. se contorsionnaient en tous sens
16. la couleur des
17. de temps à autre
18. salle de velours
19. se fige
20. sauf
21. pétrifiés
22. n'ont duré qu'
23. à demi étouffé
24. enfle

many tinted windows through which stream the rays from the tripods. But to the chamber which lies most westwardly of the seven, there are now none of the maskers[1] who venture; for[2] the night is waning away[3]; and there flows a ruddier[4] light through the blood-colored panes; and the blackness of the sable drapery[5] appals[6]; and to him whose foot falls[7] upon the sable[8] carpet, there comes from the near clock of ebony a muffled peal[9] more solemnly emphatic than any which reaches *their* ears[10] who indulge in the more remote gaieties[11] of the other apartments.

But these other apartments were densely crowded, and in them beat feverishly the heart of life. And the revel went whirlingly on[12], until at length there commenced the sounding of midnight upon the clock. And then the music ceased, as I have told; and the evolutions of the waltzers were quieted[13]; and there was an uneasy cessation of all things as before. But now there were twelve strokes to be sounded by the bell of the clock; and thus it happened, perhaps, that more of thought crept[14], with more of time, into the meditations of the thoughtful among those who revelled. And thus too, it happened, perhaps, that before the last echoes of the last chime had utterly[15] sunk into silence, there were many individuals in the crowd who had found leisure to become aware of[16] the presence of a masked figure which had arrested the attention of no single individual before. And the rumor of this new presence having spread itself whisperingly around[17], there arose at length[18] from the whole company a buzz, or murmur, expressive of disapprobation

1. personnes masquées
2. car
3. décline
4. plus fauve
5. noirceur des draperies
6. effraie
7. pour quiconque pose le pied
8. noir
9. carillon assourdi
10. les oreilles de ceux
11. s'adonnent aux festivités plus lointaines
12. tourbillon de la fête reprit
13. s'arrêtèrent
14. il se peut que davantage de pensées se soient glissées
15. complètement
16. eu le loisir de déceler
17. à voix basse
18. s'éleva enfin

and surprise—then, finally, of terror, of horror, and of disgust.

In an assembly of phantasms[1] such as I have painted, it may well be supposed that no ordinary appearance could have excited such sensation. In truth the masquerade license of the night was nearly unlimited; but the figure in question had out-Heroded Herod[2], and gone beyond the bounds[3] of even the prince's indefinite decorum. There are chords[4] in the hearts of the most reckless[5] which cannot be touched without emotion. Even with the utterly lost[6], to whom life and death are equally jests[7], there are matters of which no jest can be made. The whole company, indeed, seemed now deeply to feel that in the costume and bearing[8] of the stranger neither wit nor propriety existed[9]. The figure was tall and gaunt[10], and shrouded from head to foot in the habiliments of the grave[11]. The mask which concealed the visage was made so nearly to resemble the countenance[12] of a stiffened corpse[13] that the closest scrutiny[14] must have had difficulty in detecting the cheat[15]. And yet all this might have been endured[16], if not approved, by the mad revellers[17] around. But the mummer[18] had gone so far as to assume the type[19] of the Red Death. His vesture[20] was dabbled in[21] *blood*—and his broad brow, with all the features of the face, was besprinkled with the scarlet horror[22].

When the eyes of Prince Prospero fell upon this spectral image (which with a slow and solemn movement, as if more fully to sustain[23] its role, stalked to and fro[24] among the waltzers) he was seen to be convulsed, in the first moment

1. fantômes
2. était plus qu'excessive
3. dépassé les limites
4. cordes sensibles
5. intrépides
6. chez les plus dépravés
7. une même farce
8. l'allure
9. il n'y avait ni esprit ni bienséance
10. décharnée
11. d'un linceul
12. l'expression
13. cadavre
14. l'examen le plus attentif
15. supercherie
16. aurait pu être toléré
17. exubérants convives
18. l'intrus masqué
19. jusqu'à prendre l'aspect
20. vêtements
21. maculés de
22. aspergé de l'horrible rouge
23. comme pour mieux tenir
24. allait et venait

with a strong shudder[1] either of terror or distaste; but, in the next, his brow reddened with rage.

"Who dares?[2]" he demanded hoarsely[3] of the courtiers who stood near him—"who dares insult us with this blasphemous mockery? Seize him[4] and unmask him—that we may know whom we have to hang at sunrise, from the battlements[5]!"

It was in the eastern or blue chamber in which stood the Prince Prospero as he uttered[6] these words. They rang throughout seven rooms loudly and clearly—for the prince was a bold and robust man, and the music had become hushed[7] at the waving[8] of his hand.

It was in the blue room where stood the prince, with a group of pale courtiers by his side. At first, as he spoke, there was a slight rushing movement of this group in the direction of the intruder, who, at the moment was also near at hand, and now, with deliberate and stately[9] step, made closer approach to the speaker. But from a certain nameless awe[10] with which the mad assumptions[11] of the mummer had inspired the whole party, there were found none who put forth hand to seize him[12]; so that, unimpeded[13], he passed within a yard of the prince's person; and, while the vast assembly, as if with one impulse[14], shrank from[15] the centres of the rooms to the walls, he made his way uninterruptedly, but with the same solemn and measured step which had distinguished him from the first[16], through the blue chamber to the purple—through the purple to the green—through the green to the orange—through this again to the white—and even thence[17] to the violet, ere[18] a decided movement had been made to arrest him. It was then, however, that the Prince

1. frisson
2. Qui ose ?
3. d'une voix rauque
4. Attrapez-le
5. remparts
6. en prononçant
7. s'était tue
8. d'un geste
9. majestueux
10. en raison de la terreur indéfinissable
11. prétentions
12. il ne se trouva personne pour s'emparer de lui
13. libre de toute entrave
14. comme mue par un même élan
15. quittait
16. d'emblée
17. de là même
18. avant qu'

Prospero, maddening with[1] rage and the shame of his own momentary cowardice, rushed hurriedly through the six chambers, while none followed him on account[2] of a deadly terror that had seized upon all. He bore aloft[3] a drawn dagger[4], and had approached, in rapid impetuosity, to within three or four feet[5] of the retreating figure, when the latter[6], having attained the extremity of the velvet apartment, turned suddenly and confronted his pursuer. There was a sharp cry—and the dagger dropped gleaming[7] upon the sable carpet, upon which, instantly afterwards, fell prostrate in death[8] the Prince Prospero. Then, summoning[9] the wild courage of despair, a throng[10] of the revellers at once threw themselves into the black apartment, and, seizing the mummer, whose tall figure stood erect and motionless within the shadow of the ebony clock, gasped in unutterable horror[11] at finding the grave cerements[12] and corpse-like mask which they handled with so violent a rudeness, untenanted[13] by any tangible form.

And now was acknowledged[14] the presence of the Red Death. He had come like a thief in the night. And one by one dropped the revellers[15] in the blood-bedewed[16] halls of their revel, and died each in the despairing posture of his fall. And the life of the ebony clock went out with that of the last of the gay[17]. And the flames of the tripods expired. And Darkness and Decay[18] and the Red Death held illimitable dominion[19] over all.

1. devenant fou de

2. du fait

3. brandissait

4. poignard dégainé

5. à un bon mètre

6. celle-ci [la silhouette]

7. tomba en jetant un éclair

8. tomba mort

9. rassemblant

10. foule

11. retint un cri d'indicible terreur

12. en découvrant que le linceul

13. n'était habité

14. On reconnut alors

15. les convives tombèrent

16. [pièces] inondées de sang

17. s'éteignit avec celle du dernier de ces joyeux hôtes

18. le délabrement

19. eurent toute emprise

MS[1] FOUND IN A BOTTLE

by Edgar Allan Poe

Qui n'a plus qu'un moment à vivre
N'a plus rien à dissimuler.

Quinault, *Atys*[2]

Of my country and of my family I have little to say. Ill usage and length of years[3] have driven me[4] from the one, and estranged me from[5] the other. Hereditary wealth afforded me an education of no common order[6], and a contemplative turn of mind enabled me to methodise the stores[7] which early study very diligently garnered up[8]. Beyond all things[9], the works of the German moralists gave me great delight; not from any ill-advised[10] admiration of their eloquent madness, but from the ease with which my habits of rigid thought[11] enabled me to detect their falsities[12]. I have often been reproached with the aridity of my genius; a deficiency of imagination has been imputed to me as a crime; and the Pyrrhonism of my opinions[13] has at all times rendered me notorious. Indeed, a strong relish[14] for physical philosophy has, I fear, tinctured[15] my mind with a very common error of this age[16]—I mean the habit of referring occurrences[17], even the least susceptible of such

1. Manuscrit

2. [opéra (1676), livret de Quinault, musique de Lully]

3. La négligence et les ans

4. m'ont éloigné

5. détaché de

6. peu commune

7. fonds [de connaissance]

8. m'a permis d'engranger

9. Par-dessus tout

10. malavisée

11. tendance à la rigueur intellectuelle

12. erreurs

13. scepticisme radical

14. goût prononcé

15. imprégné

16. notre époque

17. rapporter les circonstances

reference[1], to the principles of that science. Upon the whole, no person could be less liable[2] than myself to be led away from the severe precincts[3] of truth by the *ignes fatui*[4] of superstition. I have thought proper[5] to premise thus much[6], lest[7] the incredible tale I have to tell should be considered rather the raving[8] of a crude imagination, than the positive experience of a mind to which the reveries of fancy[9] have been a dead letter and a nullity.

After many years spent in foreign travel, I sailed in the year 18—, from the port of Batavia, in the rich and populous island of Java, on a voyage to the Archipelago of the Sunda islands[10]. I went as passenger—having no other inducement[11] than a kind of nervous restlessness[12] which haunted me as a fiend[13].

Our vessel[14] was a beautiful ship of about four hundred tons, copper-fastened[15], and built at Bombay of Malabar teak[16]. She[17] was freighted with[18] cotton wool and oil, from the Lachadive[19] islands. We had also on board coir[20], jaggeree[21], ghee[22], cocoa-nuts, and a few cases of opium. The stowage was clumsily done[23], and the vessel consequently crank[24].

We got under way[25] with a mere breath of wind[26], and for many days stood along the eastern coast of Java, without any other incident to beguile[27] the monotony of our course than the occasional meeting with some of the small grabs[28] of the Archipelago to which we were bound.

One evening, leaning over the taffrail[29], I observed a very singular, isolated cloud, to the NW[30]. It was remarkable, as well for its color, as from its being the first we had seen since our departure from Batavia. I watched it attentively until

1. les plus contestables d'entre elles
2. susceptible
3. limites
4. illusions [loc. latine]
5. J'ai jugé opportun
6. fournir cette introduction
7. de crainte que
8. divagations
9. l'imagination
10. îles de la Sonde
11. motivation
12. impatience
13. démon
14. navire
15. renforcé de cuivre
16. teck
17. Il [en anglais, les embarcations sont féminisées]
18. chargé de
19. Laquedives [en Inde]
20. de la fibre de coco
21. du sucre de palme
22. du beurre clarifié
23. L'arrimage avait été mal fait
24. était mal équilibré
25. prîmes le large
26. simple brise
27. rompre
28. gourabes [navires des côtes indiennes]
29. bastingage
30. [North-West]

sunset, when it spread all at once to the eastward and westward, girting in[1] the horizon with a narrow strip of vapor, and looking like a long line of low beach[2]. My notice[3] was soon afterwards attracted by the dusky-red appearance of the moon, and the peculiar character of the sea. The latter[4] was undergoing a rapid change, and the water seemed more than usually transparent. Although I could distinctly see the bottom, yet, heaving the lead[5], I found the ship in fifteen fathoms[6]. The air now became intolerably hot, and was loaded with spiral exhalations similar to those arising from heated iron. As night came on, every breath of wind died away, and a more entire calm it is impossible to conceive. The flame of a candle burned upon the poop[7] without the least perceptible motion, and a long hair, held between the finger and thumb, hung[8] without the possibility of detecting a vibration. However, as the captain said he could perceive no indication of danger, and as we were drifting in bodily to shore[9], he ordered the sails to be furled[10], and the anchor let go[11]. No watch was set[12], and the crew[13], consisting principally of Malays, stretched themselves deliberately[14] upon deck. I went below—not without a full presentiment of evil[15]. Indeed, every appearance warranted me in apprehending a Simoon[16]. I told the captain my fears; but he paid no attention to what I said, and left me without deigning to give a reply. My uneasiness[17], however, prevented me from sleeping, and about midnight I went upon deck. As I placed my foot upon the upper step of the companion-ladder[18], I was startled by a loud, humming noise[19], like that occasioned by the rapid revolution of a mill-wheel[20],

1. ceignant
2. grève
3. attention
4. Celle-ci
5. en jetant la sonde
6. à 15 brasses [env. 25 m de fond]
7. sur la dunette
8. retombait
9. dérivions droit vers la côte
10. de serrer les voiles
11. de jeter l'ancre
12. Il n'y eut personne de quart
13. les membres de l'équipage
14. avec soin
15. mauvais pressentiment
16. tout semblait annoncer le simoun [vent violent]
17. malaise
18. l'échelle
19. puissant bourdonnement
20. roue de moulin

1. frémir en
2. tourbillon d'écume
3. nous projeta
4. sur un côté
5. d'avant en arrière
6. de la proue à la poupe
7. rafale
8. s'avéra
9. empli d'eau
10. passés par-dessus bord
11. vacillant
12. se redressa
13. Étourdi
14. en revenant à moi
15. coincé
16. l'étambot
17. le gouvernail
18. me remis sur
19. hébété,
20. des brisants
21. tourbillon
22. embarqué
23. l'appelai
24. me rejoignit à l'arrière d'un pas chancelant
25. seuls
26. ses seconds
27. inondées
28. efforts
29. cassé
30. une ficelle

and before I could ascertain its meaning, I found the ship quivering to[1] its centre. In the next instant, a wilderness of foam[2] hurled us[3] upon our beam-ends[4], and, rushing over us fore and aft[5], swept the entire decks from stem to stern[6].

The extreme fury of the blast[7] proved[8], in a great measure, the salvation of the ship. Although completely waterlogged[9], yet, as her masts had gone by the board[10], she rose, after a minute, heavily from the sea, and, staggering awhile[11] beneath the immense pressure of the tempest, finally righted[12].

By what miracle I escaped destruction, it is impossible to say. Stunned[13] by the shock of the water, I found myself, upon recovery[14], jammed in[15] between the stern-post[16] and rudder[17]. With great difficulty I gained my[18] feet, and looking dizzily[19] around, was at first struck with the idea of our being among breakers[20]; so terrific, beyond the wildest imagination, was the whirlpool[21] of mountainous and foaming ocean within which we were ingulfed. After a while, I heard the voice of an old Swede, who had shipped[22] with us at the moment of our leaving port. I hallooed to him[23] with all my strength, and presently he came reeling aft[24]. We soon discovered that we were the sole[25] survivors of the accident. All on deck, with the exception of ourselves, had been swept overboard; the captain and mates[26] must have perished as they slept, for the cabins were deluged with water[27]. Without assistance, we could expect to do little for the security of the ship, and our exertions[28] were at first paralyzed by the momentary expectation of going down. Our cable had, of course, parted[29] like pack-thread[30], at the first breath of the hurricane, or[1] we should have been instantaneously overwhelmed[2]. We scudded[3] with frightful velocity before the sea, and the water made clear breaches over us. The frame-work of our stern[4] was shattered[5] excessively, and, in almost every respect[6], we had received considerable injury[7]; but to our extreme joy we found the pumps unchoked[8], and that we had made no great shifting of our ballast[9]. The main fury of the blast had already blown over, and we apprehended little danger from the violence of the wind; but we looked forward to[10] its total cessation with dismay[11]; well believing, that in our shattered condition, we should inevitably perish in the tremendous swell[12] which would ensue[13]. But this very just apprehension seemed by no means[14] likely to be soon verified. For five entire days and nights—during which our only subsistence was a small quantity of jaggeree[15], procured with great difficulty from the forecastle[16]—the hulk flew[17] at a rate defying computation[18], before rapidly succeeding flaws of wind[19], which, without equalling the first violence of the Simoon, were still more terrific than any tempest I had before encountered. Our course[20] for the first four days was, with trifling[21] variations, SE and by S[22]; and we must have run down the coast of New Holland[23]. On the fifth day the cold became extreme, although the wind had hauled round[24] a point more to the northward. The sun arose with a sickly[25] yellow lustre, and clambered a very[26] few degrees above the horizon—emitting no decisive light. There were no clouds apparent, yet the wind was upon the increase[27], and blew with a fitful[28] and unsteady fury. About noon, as near-

1. sinon
2. submergés
3. filions
4. structure de la poupe
5. endommagée
6. à tous égards ou presque
7. subi de terribles avaries
8. que les pompes n'étaient pas engorgées
9. le lest n'avait pas trop bougé
10. attendions
11. effroi
12. houle
13. s'ensuivrait
14. nullement
15. sucre de palme
16. gaillard d'avant
17. coque fila
18. tous les calculs
19. devant la rapide succession des rafales
20. route
21. d'infimes
22. au sud-ouest quart sud
23. [l'Australie]
24. eût tourné
25. blafard
26. se hissa péniblement de
27. forcissait
28. intermittente

ly as we could guess, our attention was again arrested by the appearance of the sun. It gave out no light, properly so called, but a dull and sullen[1] glow without reflection, as if all its rays were polarized. Just before sinking within the turgid sea[2], its central fires suddenly went out, as if hurriedly extinguished by some unaccountable[3] power. It was a dim, silver-like rim[4], alone, as it rushed down the unfathomable[5] ocean.

We waited in vain for the arrival of the sixth day—that day to me has not arrived—to the Swede[6], never did arrive. Thenceforward[7] we were enshrouded in pitchy darkness[8], so that we could not have seen an object at twenty paces[9] from the ship. Eternal night continued to envelop us, all unrelieved by[10] the phosphoric sea-brilliancy to which we had been accustomed in the tropics. We observed too, that, although the tempest continued to rage with unabated[11] violence, there was no longer to be discovered the usual appearance of surf, or foam[12], which had hitherto attended us. All around were horror, and thick gloom, and a black sweltering[13] desert of ebony. Superstitious terror crept[14] by degrees into the spirit of the old Swede, and my own soul was wrapped up in silent wonder[15]. We neglected all care of the ship, as worse than useless[16], and securing ourselves[17], as well as possible, to the stump of the mizen-mast[18], looked out bitterly into the world of ocean. We had no means of calculating time, nor could we form any guess of our situation. We were, however, well aware[19] of having made farther to the southward[20] than any previous navigators, and felt great amazement at not meeting with the usual impediments[21] of ice.

1. morne
2. dans les flots boursouflés
3. inexplicable
4. Ce n'était plus qu'une faible auréole argentée
5. insondable
6. et pour le Suédois
7. Dès lors
8. plongés dans le noir absolu
9. pas
10. que n'atténuait nullement
11. incessante
12. il n'y avait plus l'habituel ressac, ni l'écume,
13. étouffant
14. s'insinuait
15. stupeur
16. comme parfaitement inutile
17. nous attachant
18. à ce qu'il restait du mât de misaine
19. conscients
20. être parvenus plus au sud
21. obstacles

In the meantime every moment threatened to be our last—every mountainous billow[1] hurried to overwhelm us. The swell surpassed anything I had imagined possible, and that we were not instantly buried[2] is a miracle. My companion spoke of the lightness of our cargo[3], and reminded me of the excellent qualities of our ship; but I could not help feeling the utter hopelessness of hope itself, and prepared myself gloomily for that death which I thought nothing could defer[4] beyond an hour, as, with every knot of way the ship made[5], the swelling of the black stupendous seas became more dismally appalling[6]. At times we gasped for breath[7] at an elevation beyond[8] the albatross—at times became dizzy with[9] the velocity of our descent into some watery hell, where the air grew stagnant, and no sound disturbed the slumbers[10] of the kraken[11].

We were at the bottom of one of these abysses, when a quick scream from my companion broke fearfully upon[12] the night. "See! see!" cried he, shrieking in my ears, "Almighty[13] God! see! see!" As he spoke, I became aware of a dull, sullen glare of red light which streamed down the sides[14] of the vast chasm[15] where we lay, and threw a fitful[16] brilliancy upon our deck. Casting my eyes upwards[17], I beheld a spectacle which froze the current of my blood[18]. At a terrific height directly above us, and upon the very verge[19] of the precipitous descent, hovered[20] a gigantic ship, of perhaps four thousand tons. Although upreared[21] upon the summit of a wave more than a hundred times her own altitude, her apparent size still exceeded that of any ship of the line[22] or East Indiaman[23] in existence. Her huge

1. vague géante
2. engloutis
3. chargement
4. différer
5. nœud que filait le navire
6. affreusement terrifiant
7. suffoquions
8. plus haute que
9. nous étions pris de vertige par
10. sommeil
11. [monstre marin des légendes scandinaves]
12. retentit lugubrement dans
13. tout-puissant
14. éclairait les flancs
15. gouffre
16. intermittente
17. Levant les yeux
18. me glaça les sangs
19. tout au bord
20. planait
21. juché
22. bâtiment de guerre
23. de tout navire commercial des Indes

hull[1] was of a deep dingy[2] black, unrelieved by any of the customary carvings[3] of a ship. A single row of brass cannon protruded from her open ports[4], and dashed[5] from their polished surfaces the fires of innumerable battle-lanterns, which swung to and fro about her rigging[6]. But what mainly inspired us with horror and astonishment, was that she bore up under a press of sail[7] in the very teeth of[8] that supernatural sea, and of that ungovernable hurricane. When we first discovered her, her bows were alone to be seen[9], as she rose slowly from the dim and horrible gulf beyond her. For a moment of intense terror she paused upon the giddy[10] pinnacle, as if in contemplation of her own sublimity, then trembled and tottered[11], and—came down.

At this instant, I know not what sudden self-possession[12] came over my spirit. Staggering as far aft[13] as I could, I awaited fearlessly the ruin that was to overwhelm[14]. Our own vessel was at length[15] ceasing from her struggles, and sinking with her head to the sea. The shock of the descending mass struck her, consequently, in that portion of her frame which was already under water, and the inevitable result was to hurl me[16], with irresistible violence, upon the rigging of the stranger[17].

As I fell, the ship hove in stays[18], and went about[19]; and to the confusion ensuing I attributed my escape from the notice[20] of the crew. With little difficulty I made my way, unperceived, to the main hatchway[21], which was partially open, and soon found an opportunity of secreting myself in the hold[22]. Why I did so I can hardly tell. An indefinite sense of awe[23], which at first sight

1. coque
2. triste et sombre
3. dépourvue des ornements ordinaires
4. sabords
5. jetaient
6. oscillaient d'avant en arrière sur ses gréements
7. il donnait pleines voiles
8. malgré
9. on ne voyait que sa proue
10. vertigineux
11. chancela
12. sang-froid
13. à l'arrière
14. désastre qui allait nous frapper
15. enfin
16. me propulser
17. vaisseau inconnu
18. fut pris vent devant
19. vira de bord
20. c'est probablement à la confusion qui s'ensuivit que je dus d'échapper à l'attention
21. écoutille
22. me cacher dans la cale
23. terreur

of the navigators of the ship had taken hold[1] of my mind, was perhaps the principle of my concealment[2]. I was unwilling to trust myself with[3] a race of people who had offered, to the cursory glance I had taken[4], so many points of vague novelty[5], doubt, and apprehension. I therefore thought proper[6] to contrive[7] a hiding-place in the hold. This I did by removing a small portion of the shifting-boards[8], in such a manner as to afford me a convenient retreat between the huge timbers[9] of the ship.

I had scarcely completed my work, when a footstep in the hold forced me to make use of it. A man passed by my place of concealment with a feeble and unsteady gait[10]. I could not see his face, but had an opportunity of observing his general appearance. There was about it an evidence of great age and infirmity. His knees tottered beneath a load of years, and his entire frame quivered under the burthen[11]. He muttered to himself, in a low broken tone, some words of a language which I could not understand, and groped[12] in a corner among a pile of singular-looking instruments, and decayed charts[13] of navigation. His manner was a wild mixture of the peevishness of second childhood[14] and the solemn dignity of a God. He at length went on deck, and I saw him no more.

A feeling, for which I have no name, has taken possession of my soul—a sensation which will admit of no analysis, to which the lessons of by-gone time[15] are inadequate, and for which I fear futurity[16] itself will offer me no key. To a mind constituted like my own, the latter consideration is an

1. s'était emparée
2. raison pour laquelle je m'étais caché
3. ne voulais pas me fier à
4. d'après le coup d'œil que j'avais jeté
5. étrangeté
6. jugeai donc préférable
7. me trouver
8. bardis [cloisonnements aménagés dans une cale]
9. membrures [poutres]
10. démarche chancelante
11. fardeau
12. fouilla à tâtons
13. de vieilles cartes
14. l'acrimonie du vieillard retombé en enfance
15. du passé
16. que l'avenir

1. très pénible
2. Je ne connaîtrai jamais, je le sais,
3. idées
4. étonnant
5. Cela fait longtemps que j'ai posé les pieds sur
6. commencent, je crois, à converger
7. Plongés
8. près de moi sans me remarquer
9. pure folie
10. ces gens ne voient pas
11. Je viens de passer
12. le second
13. là
14. ne manquerai pas d'essayer
15. le jetterai
16. une nouvelle occasion de méditer
17. pur hasard
18. cordages
19. la yole
20. Tandis que je méditais sur
21. barbouillai distraitement
22. brosse à goudron
23. bonnette [voile carrée supplémentaire]
24. tendue sur sa vergue
25. forment

evil[1]. I shall never—I know that I shall never—be satisfied with regard to[2] the nature of my conceptions[3]. Yet it is not wonderful[4] that these conceptions are indefinite, since they have their origin in sources so utterly novel. A new sense—a new entity is added to my soul.

It is long since I first trod[5] the deck of this terrible ship, and the rays of my destiny are, I think, gathering to a focus[6]. Incomprehensible men! Wrapped up[7] in meditations of a kind which I cannot divine, they pass me by unnoticed[8]. Concealment is utter folly[9] on my part, for the people *will not* see[10]. It was but just now that I passed[11] directly before the eyes of the mate[12]; it was no long while ago that I ventured into the captain's own private cabin, and took thence[13] the materials with which I write, and have written. I shall from time to time continue this journal. It is true that I may not find an opportunity of transmitting it to the world, but I will not fail to make the endeavor[14]. At the last moment I will enclose the MS in a bottle, and cast it[15] within the sea.

An incident has occurred which has given me new room for meditation[16]. Are such things the operation of ungoverned chance[17]? I had ventured upon deck and thrown myself down, without attracting any notice, among a pile of ratlin-stuff[18] and old sails, in the bottom of the yawl[19]. While musing upon[20] the singularity of my fate, I unwittingly daubed[21] with a tar-brush[22] the edges of a neatly-folded studding-sail[23] which lay near me on a barrel. The studding-sail is now bent upon the ship[24], and the thoughtless touches of the brush are spread out into[25] the word "Discovery".

I have made many observations lately upon the structure of the vessel. Although well armed, she is not, I think, a ship of war. Her rigging, build[1], and general equipment, all negative[2] a supposition of this kind. What she *is not*, I can easily perceive; what she *is*, I fear it is impossible to say. I know not how it is, but in scrutinizing[3] her strange model and singular cast of spars[4], her huge size and overgrown suits of canvass[5], her severely simple bow and antiquated stern, there will occasionally flash across my mind a sensation of familiar things, and there is always mixed up with such indistinct shadows of recollection, an unaccountable memory of old foreign chronicles and ages long ago[6].

1. sa structure
2. réfutent
3. observant
4. disposition des espars [mâts]
5. son considérable jeu de voiles
6. d'époques révolues

I have been looking at the timbers of the ship. She is built of a material to which I am a stranger. There is a peculiar character about the wood which strikes me as rendering it unfit[7] for the purpose to which it has been applied. I mean its extreme *porousness*, considered independently of the worm-eaten condition[8] which is a consequence of navigation in these seas, and apart from the rottenness attendant upon age[9]. It will appear perhaps an observation somewhat over-curious, but this wood would have every characteristic of Spanish oak, if Spanish oak were distended[10] by any unnatural means.

In reading the above sentence, a curious apothegm[11] of an old weather-beaten[12] Dutch navigator comes full upon my recollection. "It is as sure," he was wont[13] to say, when any doubt was entertained of[14] his veracity, "as sure as there is a

7. me donne à penser qu'il n'est pas fait
8. la vermoulure
9. pourriture inhérente à l'âge
10. pouvait être distendu
11. apophtegme [maxime]
12. tanné
13. avait-il coutume
14. l'on émettait quelque doute sur

1. grossira
2. me suis risqué à me glisser
3. ne m'ont prêté aucune
4. au milieu d'eux
5. sur
6. vénérable
7. courbées par la
8. peau flétrie
9. frémissait
10. tremblante
11. larmoyaient avec l'âge
12. flottaient
13. désuète
14. une bonnette qu'on avait hissée
15. courant grand largue [vent arrière toute]
16. plein
17. bardée de toute sa voilure
18. sur toute la longueur du navire
19. plongeant
20. vergues de perroquet [voile carrée placée très haut]
21. garder l'équilibre
22. ne soit pas engloutie
23. condamnés à errer
24. bord
25. Sur des flots

sea where the ship itself will grow in bulk[1] like the living body of the seaman."

About an hour ago, I made bold to thrust myself[2] among a group of the crew. They paid me no manner of[3] attention, and, although I stood in the very midst of them all[4], seemed utterly unconscious of my presence. Like the one I had at first seen in the hold, they all bore about[5] them the marks of a hoary old[6] age. Their knees trembled with infirmity; their shoulders were bent double with[7] decrepitude; their shrivelled skins[8] rattled[9] in the wind; their voices were low, tremulous[10], and broken; their eyes glistened with the rheum of years[11]; and their gray hairs streamed[12] terribly in the tempest. Around them, on every part of the deck, lay scattered mathematical instruments of the most quaint[13] and obsolete construction.

I mentioned, some time ago, the bending of a studding-sail[14]. From that period, the ship, being thrown dead off the wind[15], has continued her terrific course due[16] south, with every rag of canvass packed upon her[17], from her trucks to her lower studding-sail booms[18], and rolling[19] every moment her top-gallant yard-arms[20] into the most appalling hell of water which it can enter into the mind of man to imagine. I have just left the deck, where I find it impossible to maintain a footing[21], although the crew seem to experience little inconvenience. It appears to me a miracle of miracles that our enormous bulk is not swallowed up[22] at once and for ever. We are surely doomed to hover[23] continually upon the brink[24] of eternity, without taking a final plunge into the abyss. From billows[25] a thousand times more stupendous than any I have ever seen, we glide away with the facility of the arrowy sea-gull[1]; and the colossal waters rear[2] their heads above us like demons of the deep, but like demons confined to[3] simple threats, and forbidden to destroy. I am led to attribute these frequent escapes to the only natural cause which can account for such effect. I must suppose the ship to be within the influence of some strong current, or impetuous under-tow[4].

I have seen the captain face to face, and in his own cabin—but, as I expected, he paid me no attention. Although in his appearance there is, to a casual observer[5], nothing which might bespeak him[6] more or less than man, still, a feeling of irrepressible reverence and awe mingled with the sensation of wonder[7] with which I regarded him. In stature, he is nearly my own height; that is, about five feet eight inches[8]. He is of a well-knit and compact frame of body[9], neither robust nor remarkable otherwise. But it is the singularity of the expression which reigns upon the face—it is the intense, the wonderful, the thrilling evidence of old age, so utter[10], so extreme, which excites within my spirit a sense—a sentiment ineffable. His forehead, although little wrinkled[11], seems to bear upon it the stamp of a myriad of years. His gray hairs are records of the past, and his grayer eyes are sybils of the future[12]. The cabin floor was thickly strewn with[13] strange, iron-clasped folios[14], and mouldering[15] instruments of science, and obsolete long-forgotten charts. His head was bowed down upon his hands, and he pored, with a fiery, unquiet eye, over[16] a paper which I took

1. d'une mouette en plein vol
2. dressent
3. voués à n'être que de
4. courant sous-marin
5. à première vue
6. puisse indiquer qu'il soit
7. d'étonnement
8. environ 1,80 m
9. ossature compacte
10. entière
11. ridé
12. semblent deviner l'avenir
13. jonché d'
14. volumes à fermoirs en fer
15. moisis
16. fixait d'un œil ardent et inquiet

to be a commission, and which, at all events[1], bore the signature of a monarch. He muttered to himself—as did the first seaman whom I saw in the hold—some low peevish[2] syllables of a foreign tongue; and although the speaker was close at my elbow[3], his voice seemed to reach my ears from the distance of a mile.

1. en tout cas
2. acerbes
3. tout près de moi

The ship and all in it are imbued with the spirit of Eld[4]. The crew glide to and fro[5] like the ghosts of buried centuries; their eyes have an eager and uneasy meaning[6]; and when their fingers fall athwart my path in[7] the wild glare of the battle-lanterns, I feel as I have never felt before, although I have been all my life a dealer in antiquities, and have imbibed the[8] shadows of fallen columns at Balbec, and Tadmor, and Persepolis, until my very soul[9] has become a ruin.

4. temps jadis
5. vont et viennent
6. expression avide et agitée
7. croisent mon chemin sous
8. que je me sois imprégné des
9. âme elle-même

When I look around me, I feel ashamed of my former apprehensions. If I trembled at the blast which has hitherto attended us[10], shall I not stand aghast[11] at a warring[12] of wind and ocean, to convey any idea of which,[13] the words tornado and simoon are trivial[14] and ineffective? All in the immediate vicinity of the ship, is the blackness of eternal night, and a chaos of foamless water; but, about a league[15] on either side of us, may be seen, indistinctly and at intervals, stupendous ramparts of ice, towering away into[16] the desolate sky, and looking like the walls of the universe.

10. nous a secoués jusqu'à présent
11. ne devrais-je pas être frappé de terreur
12. par le combat
13. dont, pour en donner une idée,
14. insignifiants
15. lieue [env. 4 km]
16. dressés haut vers

As I imagined, the ship proves[17] to be in a current—if that appellation can properly be given to

17. s'avère

a tide[1] which, howling and shrieking by the white ice, thunders on to the southward[2] with a velocity like the headlong dashing[3] of a cataract.

1. marée
2. fonce à grand fracas vers le sud
3. chutes vertigineuses

To conceive the horror of my sensations is, I presume, utterly impossible; yet a curiosity to penetrate the mysteries of these awful regions, predominates even over my despair, and will reconcile me to the most hideous aspect of death. It is evident that we are hurrying onwards to some exciting knowledge[4]—some never-to-be-imparted[5] secret, whose attainment is[6] destruction. Perhaps this current leads us to the southern pole itself. It must be confessed that a supposition apparently so wild has every probability in its favor.

4. savoir
5. inviolable
6. qui ne se réalisera que par la

The crew pace[7] the deck with unquiet and tremulous step; but there is upon their countenances[8] an expression more of the eagerness[9] of hope than of the apathy of despair.

In the meantime the wind is still in our poop[10], and, as we carry a crowd of canvass[11], the ship is at times lifted bodily[12] from out the sea! Oh, horror upon horror!—the ice opens suddenly to the right, and to the left, and we are whirling dizzily[13], in immense concentric circles, round and round the borders of a gigantic amphitheatre, the summit of whose walls is lost in the darkness and the distance. But little time will be left me to ponder upon[14] my destiny! The circles rapidly grow small—we are plunging madly within the grasp[15] of the whirlpool—and amid a roaring,

7. arpentent
8. visages
9. force
10. arrière
11. multitude de voiles
12. se soulève parfois
13. nous nous mettons à tournoyer vertigineusement
14. il ne me reste guère de temps pour songer à
15. à portée

1. le grondement, le mugissement et le bruit tonitruant
2. tremble

and bellowing, and thundering[1] of ocean and of tempest, the ship is quivering[2]—oh God! and — going down!

Note.—The "MS Found in a Bottle," was originally published in 1831; and it was not until many years afterwards that I became acquainted with the[3] maps of Mercator, in which the ocean is represented as rushing, by four mouths[4], into the (northern) Polar Gulf, to be absorbed into the bowels[5] of the earth; the Pole itself being represented by a black rock, towering to a prodigious height.

3. j'eus connaissance des
4. embouchures
5. entrailles

Table of contents

La collection Yes you can!

Les faux débutants

Linwood Barclay *Broken Promise*

M. C. Beaton *Agatha Raisin and the Quiche of Death*

Harlan Coben *The Stranger*

Michael Connelly *The Black Box*

Michael Connelly *The Burning Room*

Michael Connelly *The Drop*

Michael Connelly *The Wrong Side of Goodbye*

Ken Follett *The Modigliani Scandal*

Mary Higgins Clark *A Cry in the Night*

Mary Higgins Clark *A Stranger is Watching*

Mary Higgins Clark *Loves Music, Loves to Dance*

Mary Higgins Clark *Where are the Children?*

Anthony Horowitz *The House of Silk*

Ian Rankin *Knots & Crosses*

Nicholas Sparks *Message in a Bottle*

Les intermédiaires

Harlan Coben *Caught*

Harlan Coben *Play Dead*

Harlan Coben *Stay Close*

Harlan Coben *Tell No One*

Harlan Coben *The Woods*

Ken Follett *Paper Money*

Anthony Horowitz *Moriarty*

P. D. James *A Mind to Murder*

P. D. James *Death Comes to Pemberley*

Douglas Kennedy *The Big Picture*

Stephen King *Finders Keepers*

Stephen King	*The Green Mile*
John le Carré	*A Most Wanted Man*
Yann Martel	*Life of Pi*

Les avancés

Paul Auster	*Leviathan*
Paul Auster	*Oracle Night*
Julian Barnes	*The Sense of an Ending*
Michael Cunningham	*By Nightfall*
Michael Cunningham	*The Hours*
Helen Fielding	*Bridget Jones's Diary*
Helen Fielding	*Bridget Jones: The Edge of Reason*
Elizabeth George	*A Great Deliverance*
Stephen King	*Dolores Claiborne*
Stephen King	*Misery*

Les classiques

Jane Austen	*Pride and Prejudice*
G. K. Chesterton	*The Innocence of Father Brown*
Arthur Conan Doyle	*The Hound of the Baskervilles*
Francis Scott Fitzgerald	*Tender is the Night*
Francis Scott Fitzgerald	*The Great Gatsby*
Washington Irving, Arthur Conan Doyle, Edgar Allan Poe	*The Legend of Sleepy Hollow and Other Scary Stories*
Edgar Allan Poe	*The Fall of the House of Usher and Other Stories*
Mary Shelley	*Frankenstein*
Bram Stoker	*Dracula*
Edith Wharton	*The Age of Innocence*
Oscar Wilde	*The Importance of Being Earnest*
Oscar Wilde	*The Picture of Dorian Gray*
Virginia Woolf	*To the Lighthouse*

HARRAP s'engage pour l'environnement en réduisant l'empreinte carbone de ses livres. Celle de cet exemplaire est de :
350 g éq. CO_2
Rendez-vous sur www.larousse-durable.fr

PAPIER À BASE DE FIBRES CERTIFIÉES

Imprimé en Italie par Grafica Veneta
Dépôt légal : août 2019
323916-01/11041365 - août 2019